"I'm not very strong, mister. You could probably tell that. Don't think I'd be much help to you."

"Well, maybe you could pick my garden for me."

"I might could do that." But what would happen when he found out she wasn't a boy or a young man? Samantha let out a deep breath and took off her smoke-filled hat. She pulled out the pin holding up her hair, and the mass of blond hair tumbled down around her shoulders. "I'm not what you think."

His eyes widened as he nodded. "I can see you're not. Well, I guess you're right. With no woman around, I couldn't ask you to stay at my place. And my neighbor's wife is out of town, so his place wouldn't work either."

"Thanks anyway," Samantha said. "At least I still have my horse and a little money to eat on."

"Listen, I'm headed into Guthrie now. My sister has a boardinghouse—let me take you to her place. Even if she doesn't have an opening, she may know someone who does."

For the first time in days, Samantha felt a glimmer of hope.

JANET LEE BARTON and her husband, Dan, have recently moved to Oklahoma and feel blessed to have at least one daughter and her family living nearby. Janet loves being able to share her faith and love of the Lord through her writing. She's very happy that the kind of romances the Lord has called her to write can be read by and shared with women of all ages.

Books by Janet Lee Barton

HEARTSONG PRESENTS

HP434—Family Circle
HP532—A Promise Made
HP562—Family Ties
HP623—A Place Called Home
HP644—Making Amends
HP689—Unforgettable
HP710—To Love Again
HP730—With Open Arms
HP745—Family Reunion
HP759—Stirring Up Romance
HP836—A Love for Keeps
HP852—A Love All Her Own
HP868—A Love to Cherish
HP956—I'd Sooner Have Love

Sooner
Sunrise

Janet Lee Barton

Heartsong Presents

To Dan who has encouraged and read for me from the beginning, to Nicole who reads even when she's sleep deprived, to the rest of our wonderful family who always encourage me, and especially to our Lord and Savior for showing me the way. I love you all with all my heart.

A note from the Author:
I love to hear from my readers! You may correspond with me by writing:

Janet Lee Barton
Author Relations
PO Box 721
Uhrichsville, OH 44683

ISBN 978-1-61626-494-9

SOONER SUNRISE

All scripture quotations are taken from the King James Version of the Bible.

This book is a work of fiction. Names, characters, places, and incidents are either products of the author's imagination or used fictitiously.

Our mission is to publish and distribute inspirational products offering exceptional value and biblical encouragement to the masses.

PRINTED IN THE U.S.A.

one

Ben Thompson loved the sunrises that came up over the land he farmed, nestled near a creek midway between Guthrie and Edmond Station. He took a swig of coffee as he waited for the sun to rise over one of the nearby hills, spreading the light of day over his fields. Leaning against the porch railing, he watched the world come awake around him.

The sun rose over the knoll and began to chase the last of the darkness away. A rooster crowed, announcing daylight's arrival, and in the distance, his neighbor's cows lowed.

It promised to be a beautiful day, and Ben was happy it was Friday. He'd pick the ripest vegetables and fruits in his garden to take into Guthrie when he went to see his children for the weekend. He sorely missed Hope and Matt, but Faith had been right. They needed schooling, and with no wife to help teach them out here, the best place for them during the school year was with his sister and her husband in Guthrie.

Rose, the owner of the farm he managed, had insisted that he add a couple of rooms to the small house her late husband had built. With his brother-in-law and Matt's help, each of his children now had a room of their own when they stayed with him.

To Ben, this place was the prettiest spot in Oklahoma

5

Territory, and he'd about decided that if Rose was willing to sell to him, he was ready to buy her out. If not, he'd keep farming because he loved doing it better than anything else he'd tried. Still, he missed his children. And he missed his Molly—even though the memories of what she looked like were beginning to fade. If not for the small picture he carried with him, he was afraid he'd forget her sweet face altogether.

Thankfully, he still saw her in Hope's smile and Matt's eyes. And he could see her in some of their actions. The way Hope set herself to finish any task given to her as well as she could and the way she put her hands on her hips when she was put out at her brother. He saw Molly in Matt when he showed patience with his sister and in the easy way he caught on to nearly any new project that came along.

But seeing Molly in their children wasn't the same as having her with him, and Ben was about as lonely as a body could be. He took a last swig from his cup and set it down on the porch to take care of later. For now, he needed to pick his garden and add to what he'd picked the day before. He had enough vegetables to sell to several of the grocers and restaurants in town and still have some left over to take to his sister. She had a nice little garden, but trying to provide meals for her boarders on a daily basis required more vegetables than her small lot could produce.

The sun was high when Ben finished filling his baskets and loading them in the wagon. He went inside and cleaned up a bit before making sure everything was locked up until his return.

After hitching his horse, Rusty, up to the wagon, he pulled out of his place and headed toward town, stopping first to make sure his closest neighbor knew he'd be gone.

Homer Barnett ambled out of his barn to meet Ben. His wife had taken the children and gone back East to visit her parents for a while, and he was about as lonesome as Ben was.

"Mornin', Homer. Will you mind watching the place while I'm in town for the weekend?"

Homer pushed his hat back on his head and looked up at him. "I'll be glad to. It'll give me somethin' to do with the family gone."

"I sure do appreciate it, Homer. Is there anything I can bring back from town for you?"

"Maybe a newspaper or two. I kind of like knowin' what's going on in Guthrie. Lots of news coming out of there, what with it becoming the territorial capital and the governor arriving next week."

"That's true. There's supposed to be all kinds of celebrations in town, from what my sister has told me. I don't know if I'll go in next week. Sure you don't want to go in with me today? I'm sure our places will be fine for a day or two."

Homer shook his head. "Nah. I don't much like all those crowds in town. But I sure do like readin' about it all."

"Okay, then I'll be sure to pick up those papers for you. I'll be back Sunday evening or Monday morning like usual." Ben often waited until Monday to come back. It gave him one less night by himself.

"No need to hurry if you decide to stay for those celebrations. I'll be here."

Ben reached down and shook Homer's hand. "Thank you, Homer."

Homer nodded, and Ben flicked the reins to his wagon. It was a relief to know he had someone to look after the place. Like Homer, he wasn't thrilled about the crowds in Guthrie, but it was where his family lived, and he couldn't wait to see them. Faith would have one of his favorite meals for supper that night—and all weekend, most likely—even though she had a new husband to take into account now. But Gabe liked anything Faith cooked, and Ben was sure he wouldn't be complaining if she fixed her brother a few of his favorite meals.

He looked forward to hearing all the news, too, but while he liked visiting Guthrie, he loved living on the farm. Lately though, he'd been wishing he had someone to share his life with, someone to talk to of an evening, to wake up with of a morning and share that sunrise over a cup of coffee. But his life was what it was, and he'd best be counting his many blessings instead of yearning for more.

That was easier said than done some days. Today was better—he'd be with family. But after seeing how happy Faith and Gabe were, well, he had to admit he was a little envious, and he had to ask for the Lord's forgiveness for that often. Truth was, seeing them together made him long even more for a wife to share his life with.

It didn't look like that was very likely to happen—not with him living out on the farm and only going to town on weekends. Even if he didn't spend most of that time with his family, Ben wouldn't have an overabundance of single women to pick from in Guthrie—and those who were available either weren't the kind he'd be marrying, or they were snapped up before he had a chance to find them. He'd best be content with the life he had. If he was ever to marry again, the good Lord would have to bring the right woman to him.

Ben's gaze roamed the countryside as he traveled. He looked to the northeast and for a moment he thought he caught a whiff of smoke. It was probably someone making breakfast at their campsite. But as he continued on and the smell got stronger, he could see the smoke was from more than just a campfire. He set Rusty into a run.

※

Samantha Carter took another sip of coffee. It wasn't too bad this morning. Maybe she was getting the hang of camping— she should. Her brother had taught her how to cook over a campfire and how to pitch a tent at an early age. He'd taught her to fish and how to shoot a gun. But she'd never quite gotten the hang of hunting—if she had, she'd be eating real well out here. Still, it wasn't the kind of life she envisioned when she left Kansas more than a week ago.

She didn't know what good it would do, but she'd go into Guthrie one more time to try to find work and a place to live. With it being such a new town, she hadn't thought she'd have any problem finding employment when she chose it as her destination. But evidently she was wrong. The only kind of work that seemed available was the kind she wasn't going to take.

And as for a place to live—it seemed every hotel room in the town was taken up with either people waiting to get a house built or those who came in to celebrate Guthrie becoming the territorial capital. All kinds of celebrations were planned for May 23, when the new governor would be arriving. Maybe a room would be available once that was all done with, but since that was still a week away, she was thinking maybe she ought to go on to Edmond Station and see what was there. If that didn't work, maybe Oklahoma City would have more opportunities. She'd heard that it was growing faster than Guthrie now.

Samantha only wanted to be settled and quit having to

wear boys' clothing—that was the only size she could get to pass as a man. Thankfully, she hadn't been bothered by anyone. But a woman out here alone on the prairie. . . well, she'd seen what a man could try with a woman alone anywhere, and she wanted all the protection she could get. Samantha poured what little was left of her coffee on the campfire and shoved some dirt over it with her boot before heading down to the small creek behind her tent to wash her face and put her hair back up under the hat that helped hide the fact that she was a woman.

It'd been a still morning, cool and dry just the way she liked. After scrubbing her face, she twisted her hair and pinned it up before putting her hat back on. Leaning back on her elbows, she gazed at the big puffs of white clouds while she tried to talk herself into going back to Guthrie, even though she really didn't think she had any chance of finding a job there. The clouds seemed to be moving faster than usual. Then she caught a whiff of the smell of something burning. Sam turned and looked in horror as a sudden breeze sent sparks to her tent from the fire she'd thought she'd put out. Small flames began licking one side of the tent.

She took off running, her heart pounding harder with each step she took. About everything she owned was in that tent. *Dear Lord, please don't let me lose it all!* By the time she reached the only shelter she had, the flames had grown larger and threatened to engulf one side. She ran through the flap and was overwhelmed by smoke. Coughing, she managed to get the saddlebag that carried what little money she had and get it out. She was just about to go back in, when she was yanked to a stop.

"Whoa, there! You can't be goin' back inside, son," a deep

voice said from behind her.

Samantha twisted and kicked against his firm hold. "But I have to—everything I have—"

"Nothing in there can be that important. That tent is about to be devoured any minute now." Samantha struggled for only a few more moments before she saw the flames reach the top of the tent and exactly as the man had predicted, quickly devour the rest of the structure. The strong arms eased their hold of her, and the man who'd held her back began to stomp the fire out around the perimeter of the tent. Sam did the same, but it seemed to do no good. She picked up the coffeepot she'd emptied earlier and ran to the creek to fill it. She poured it over the embers and then rushed back to the creek for more. At least the source of the fire was out. She went to fill the pot one more time, and when she got back, the man used it to snuff out the few hot spots left. Together they made sure no live embers remained.

"Good thing we had a rain a few days ago." The man turned to her and let out a deep breath. "I'm sorry, son. But I couldn't let you go back in there. What's your name?"

She hesitated for a moment and remembered to lower her voice. "Name's Sam Carter."

"Nice to meet you, Sam. I'm Ben Thompson." He motioned to the south. "I farm down the road. Where are you headed anyway?"

"I've been looking for work in Guthrie, but there's not much there."

"Well, I might could use some help on my farm for a bit, at least until you can figure out what to do next. It's only me though, and I'm not a great cook, but it'd be better than nothing at all."

Samantha let out a deep breath. Even if she did know something about farming, she couldn't take him up on his offer—he was under the impression she was a young man, and there really wasn't any way she could keep her secret from him if she stayed on his place.

"Thanks, but I don't know anything about farming." Didn't really want to know anything about it either.

"I can teach you what you need to know."

"I appreciate it, but—"

"But what?" The man stood with his hands on his hips as if he was wondering why someone who needed a job would turn an offer down.

"I'm not very strong, mister. You could probably tell that. Don't think I'd be much help to you."

"Well, maybe you could pick my garden for me."

"I might could do that." But what would happen when he found out she wasn't a boy or a young man? Samantha let out a deep breath and took off her smoke-filled hat. She pulled out the pin holding up her hair, and the mass of blond hair tumbled down around her shoulders. "I'm not what you think."

His eyes widened as he nodded. "I can see you're not. Well, I guess you're right. With no woman around, I couldn't ask you to stay at my place. And my neighbor's wife is out of town, so his place wouldn't work either."

"Thanks anyway," Samantha said. "At least I still have my horse and a little money to eat on."

"Listen, I'm headed into Guthrie now. My sister has a boardinghouse—let me take you to her place. Even if she doesn't have an opening, she may know someone who does."

For the first time in days, Samantha felt a glimmer of

hope. Besides, she really didn't have a choice unless she wanted to sleep in the elements. She nodded. "I'd appreciate that."

The man held out his hand. "Pleased to make your acquaintance, uh. . .Sam."

Samantha hesitated for a moment. She didn't trust men anymore, but this one had saved her life. She slipped her hand in his. "I'm Samantha Carter. I. . .thank you for—"

He waved her thanks away. "I'm thankful you weren't hurt. I am sorry for your loss, though. Maybe my sister will have something you can wear. Let me tie your horse to my wagon, and we'll be on our way."

Samantha was glad he was there to get her horse under control. It had been spooked by the fire and was a little hard to calm down. But it didn't take long for Mr. Thompson to get him settled. While he was doing that, Samantha grabbed her saddlebag and the towel she'd taken to the river. The hat she left behind, as it smelled of smoke. She was sure her hair did too, but she couldn't do anything about that at present. Maybe she could take a real bath at Mr. Thompson's sister's place. She sure hoped so.

❧

Hard as he tried, Ben couldn't keep from stealing glances at the young woman sitting beside him. He'd thought the young man she'd posed as was a little on the small side and even wondered if he could do the work needed at the farm. Now he knew why. She was a small woman, and he felt sure that the clothes she wore were boys'. She'd probably dressed that way for her own protection, and it was a good idea—he'd give that to her. But there'd be no need to dress like a man at Faith's. He hoped his sister had something she could wear.

"I suppose you're wondering what I was doing camping out or even if I was trying to jump a claim."

Ben suppressed a chuckle. No bigger than she was, he didn't think she'd be able to hold a claim, should she try to jump it, but he had a feeling she wouldn't take well to him saying it. "No, ma'am. Most places have been claimed by now, and all the neighbors around know whose claim is whose. I take people at their word, and if you came to find work here, that's what I believe. I'm sorry you haven't had much luck at it. My sister, Faith, might know of something, though. She and her husband know a lot of people in town now."

"That would be wonderful. If not, I suppose I'll try Edmond Station or even Oklahoma City."

"Hopefully, there won't be any need for that." Ben didn't like the idea of her taking off on her own. It wasn't safe for a woman to be out here alone—something she was obviously aware of. And she didn't even have anything to camp out in. He flicked the reins and set Rusty to a canter. He'd drop Miss Carter off at the boardinghouse and put her in Faith's care until he could get back from delivering his produce. Somehow, they had to find a way to help her.

When they entered Guthrie, he was surprised by the increased traffic from a week ago. Evidently all this territorial stuff was more important than he'd first thought. "It is more crowded than usual. I can see why it was hard to find a place to stay."

"I didn't realize all this would be going on right now. I just wanted..."

Ben wondered if she'd stopped midsentence because she didn't want to tell him what it was she wanted. He hadn't run across many women who came to the territory alone. And that made it even more dangerous in some ways for Miss Carter to be out here alone. Faith would take her in. That he had no doubt of. And it was a good thing, too, because no way would he leave this young woman in town otherwise.

"I'd heard that Guthrie turned into a city overnight, but I don't think I believed it until I arrived. How long have you been in the territory?" Miss Carter asked.

"I came in that first day." Ben chuckled. "It became a city of tents by nightfall, and it was one big mess. People were staking claims all over the place, even in the middle of some streets."

"It must have been exciting." Miss Carter's blue eyes crinkled at the corners as she smiled. "If I'd have come then, I might have a place to stay now."

"You might. Then again—those first few days were trying. Oh, it was exciting, but a day or two after we got here, the wind kicked up the dust, and then the rain came, and we had to deal with mud everywhere. Not easy when you're living in a wagon or tent. But that's probably why so many buildings went up as fast as they did. No one wanted to be caught like that again."

"And it's gone from tents to this in barely a year?" Miss Carter waved her right hand to call notice to the buildings they were passing.

"It did. And in another year's time, it will be even harder to recognize from those first days." Ben had a hard time remembering what it looked like last year. If not for the photographs taken by the reporters who'd come from all over the country, no one would believe how quickly Guthrie had become a real city. "Every time I come into town, I see new buildings. No tents now and most of the frame buildings will be gone by this time next year."

He pointed out a couple of buildings going up on Second Street. "That's the DeFord Building, and the one down the way is the Bonfils Building. Joseph Foucart is building them. I hear he's a famous architect from Belgium."

"They are going to be quite beautiful when they are finished. They're quite ornate, with all the brick and stone, and his designs are very unique and quite elegant." Miss Carter said, craning her head as Ben passed them by.

"Yes, they are. My brother-in-law is quite a good builder, too. He builds mostly homes, but he's also built a few businesses in town. He built my sister's boardinghouse before they got married," Ben said as he continued down Second Street to Noble. He pulled his wagon into the yard between two lots.

"Oh, is this your sister's boardinghouse?" Miss Carter asked. "I don't think she's going to have a place for me. I already tried here. But the lady who answered the door said they were full up." She looked at Ben. "She was older—"

"Oh, that must have been Rose or maybe one of the boarders. She probably is full up, but I know my sister will make room for you." He jumped down, came around the wagon, and held out his hand. "Come on. Come meet Faith."

two

Samantha took the hand he offered and stepped down from the wagon. She wasn't sure why, but she felt nervous about meeting this sister of Mr. Thompson's. It was probably because she was still dressed as a man—or boy—and she reeked of smoke. She reached up and touched her hair. No telling what it looked like and—

"Don't worry. Faith will get you cleaned up in no time, and you'll feel more yourself."

How did he know she was feeling so insecure? Probably from the smell and the look of her, Samantha decided as she let him lead her to the front door of the boardinghouse.

He didn't knock, just opened the door and went inside, calling, "Faith, Matt, Hope!"

Footsteps came from the back of the house, and a woman about Samantha's age with blue eyes and beautiful auburn hair, bearing a definite resemblance to Mr. Thompson, hurried to the front hall, wiping her hands on an apron.

"Ben! You're here early!" She hugged him and then gave him a tap on the shoulder with her fist. "And you know Matt and Hope are still at school this time of day."

Only then did she turn to Samantha. "And who is this you have with you?" Her eyes were kind, and her smile bright.

Samantha cringed at what she must think of her, all smoky and—

"Sis, this is Miss Samantha Carter, and she's not had a

good start to her day. She was camping between here and my place when her tent caught on fire this morning. She's lost near everything she owns. Faith, I'm hoping you can help her out. Miss Carter, this is my sister, Faith Logan."

Samantha could see the compassion in Mrs. Logan's eyes as she reached out and put a hand on her shoulder. "I'm so sorry about your loss, Miss Carter. Come, let me fix you a cup of tea, and we'll figure out what to do."

Before Samantha knew what happened, she was sitting at a table in a sunny kitchen, and Mr. Thompson was leaning against the doorframe explaining how he found her, while his sister made her a cup of tea.

"Oh, I'm so glad Ben came by when he did, Miss Carter," Mrs. Logan said.

"Yes, I am, too." Samantha stole a glance at Mr. Thompson and saw that he was studying her intently, with a look of concern in his eyes. Suddenly it hit her that the man had actually saved her life. If he hadn't stopped her, she would have run back into the tent. "I'm very beholden to him."

Mr. Thompson pushed away from the doorframe and stood straight. He shook his head. "I didn't do anything anyone else wouldn't have done. I'm glad the good Lord put me in the right place at the right time."

Faith Logan put a cup of tea down on the table in front of Samantha and turned to her brother. "You want some coffee?"

"No, not now. I've got to deliver my produce to some of the stores in town. I'll leave yours on the back porch and bring it in when I get back. I wanted to get Miss Carter here first. I won't be long. She's in need of work and a place to stay. She actually came here the other day, and Rose or one or your boarders told her you were full up—but I'm hoping we can find a place for her to sleep and eat, at least until she can find something more permanent."

"Don't worry, Ben. We'll figure out something. You go on and take care of business, and I'll take care of Miss Carter."

Samantha felt like a bystander as the two talked around her. But she sensed that they really cared, and she didn't have many options, anyway. So she said, "Thank you. I'm sorry to be so much trouble."

"You aren't any trouble at all," Mrs. Logan said with a smile. "Now go on, Ben. I'm thinking Miss Carter would like to get some of that smoke and ash off of her and her clothing."

He hesitated long enough that his sister gave him a once-over and said, "You know you could use a little cleaning up, yourself."

"I'll use the pump outside."

His sister nodded. "That will help. You have some soot on your cheek."

"Thanks for pointin' it out, sis."

Mrs. Logan laughed. "You're welcome. Go on, now. We'll see you after a while."

"You're all right with this?" Ben Thompson looked into Samantha's eyes, and her heart stirred at the caring tone in his voice.

"Yes, I'm fine with it. Thank you—"

He waved away her thanks and headed for the back door. "I'll see you both later."

Faith Logan shook her head. "He'll be chomping at the bit to get back here and see how you are." She turned to Samantha. "Come on with me. I'll run you a hot bath and find you something to change in to. We're about the same size so it shouldn't be a problem."

She never asked why Samantha was dressed in boys' clothing, never asked where she'd come from. She simply led her back to a real bathroom with a huge, claw-footed tub and began to run water. In all her twenty-five years, Samantha didn't think she'd ever been accepted so readily.

"There's soap right there, and if you take off your clothes and leave them outside the door, I'll get them washed."

"Oh I can do that—"

"You can help later. For now, I'll find you something of mine to wear and have it all right outside. Don't worry about being interrupted. It's only women here this time of day, and this is my bathroom, so no one should bother you."

"Thank you, Mrs. Logan."

"You're welcome. And please call me Faith."

"If you'll call me Samantha."

Faith grinned and nodded. "Have a good soak, Samantha." She slipped out the door, and Samantha sighed in anticipation of the first long, hot soak she'd had in days.

❧

Trying to keep his mind off the woman he'd just left at his sister's wasn't an easy feat as Ben went about his business, delivering his produce. His normal deliveries were to the Diamond Grocery on the corner of Cleveland and Sixth Streets, Allen & Anderson on the corner of Fifth and Vilas, and Kimbal Grocery and Provision on Division Street. After that, he checked in with several new grocers to see if they would buy from him. The town didn't lack for grocers or any other kind of store, for that matter.

Once in a while he wondered if he'd done the right thing

by leasing Rose's farm and not staying in town to work with his brother-in-law. But every day brought something more to do on the farm, and deep in his heart, Ben knew he wouldn't be happy living in town for long. He liked the open spaces and the peace and quiet of his farm. Still, it might be a sight easier to find someone to share his life with here in town.

Then again, the only single woman he'd come across in a long time was Samantha Carter, and the only thing he was pretty certain about her was that she wasn't *that* kind of woman—if so, she'd have found work in a hurry.

He couldn't help but wonder what she'd look like all cleaned up. She had the prettiest blue eyes he'd ever seen, and in the sunlight, her hair lit up like spun gold, even smelling of smoke and with bits of ash in it. For some reason, the name *Sam* fit her, at least what he'd seen of her so far. She had a lot of spunk to be out here alone. He had to give that much to her.

Ben pulled out his pocket watch. They'd gotten into town right after noon, and his stomach was growling like nobody's business. But he didn't want to bother Faith for something to eat midafternoon. Besides, he knew she didn't want him back until Miss Carter had a chance to clean up. He'd grab something at one of the eateries in town, and then he'd head back to the boardinghouse.

He stopped at the Oklahoma Café on East Oklahoma and found one empty table. It didn't seem to matter what time of day it was—all the cafés in town did a good business. Many men like him were bound to get sick and tired of their own cooking. If it wasn't for the food Faith insisted he take back to the farm with him, he'd probably be riding into town more often than on weekends. His cooking left a lot to be desired.

"What'll ya have?" the proprietor asked. "We have stew and beans today. Served with corn bread. Take your pick."

"I'll have the stew." He'd seen a plate of beans delivered to the next table, and they sure didn't look like his sister's. He could only hope the stew looked better.

"It'll be right out."

Ben looked around and saw mostly men in the place, which wasn't unusual for the new town. Many men had come in to get settled before sending for their families. He wondered if any of them had wives still waiting back wherever they came from, or if like him, they wished for someone to share their life with.

His stew arrived steaming hot with a big slab of corn bread. He bowed his head and said a silent blessing before taking his first bite. It wasn't nearly as good as his sister's stew, but it was better than he could cook, and it would serve the purpose and keep his stomach from growling at her supper table.

By the time he finished, it was nearly time for his children to get out of school. He decided he'd buy some newspapers for Homer and swing by the school to get Matt and Hope. Then they'd go back to Faith's, and he'd see how well Miss Carter had cleaned up.

He purchased the papers at a newsstand that had recently opened up on the corner and put them under the wagon seat. Then he went to get his children. As he waited outside the schoolhouse, he found it hard to believe that Hope had just turned fourteen. And Matt was now fifteen. They were growing up on him way too fast. It seemed only yesterday—

The school bell rang, and in minutes, children were swarming out the door. Hope was outside before Matt, and she was talking to another girl about her age when Matt joined them. They turned in his direction, and Ben's heart swelled at the smiles that broke out when his children recognized him.

"Papa!" Hope took off in a run, and Matt hurried his long stride. Ben jumped down from the wagon and swung Hope up into a hug. He set her down and turned to give a manly hug to his son. "It's good to see the two of you! I'm sure ready for the harvest break to get here, already."

Ben wondered about the look Matt and Hope exchanged as Hope climbed up onto the seat up front by her father and Matt jumped in the back.

"It'll be here before we know it, Papa," Hope said.

"And I can't wait!" Matt settled up near the wagon seat and held on to the back of it. "I'm eager to get out to the farm for more than a few days at a time."

"In the meantime, I'm so glad you are here, Papa," Hope said.

"So am I, darlin'. I had quite an adventure today."

"Oh? What happened?" Matt asked.

Ben told them about the fire and Miss Carter. "She lost everything she had, which probably wasn't much, so you two be extra nice and considerate of her, okay?"

"Oh how sad," Hope said. "Of course we will, Papa."

"Boy, it's a good thing you came along when you did, Papa," Matt said. "She might have died in that tent if you hadn't been there to keep her out of it."

Ben shuddered thinking about it. He wanted no credit for saving her—instead he sent up a silent thank-you that with the Lord's help he'd been able to keep that tragedy from happening.

Samantha didn't get out of the tub until the water turned cool. She couldn't remember when she'd enjoyed a bath more. Faith's dress fit her perfectly, and Samantha loved the material, which matched the blue of the sky on a fall day. She always felt good when wearing that particular shade. She'd washed the smoky smell out of her hair, and it dried in natural curls that she put up on top of her head.

By the time she made her way back to the kitchen, she felt like herself for the first time since she'd left Kansas. Faith was checking something that smelled like roast chicken in the oven and talking to another woman who looked up from icing a cake. She appeared to be in her late forties or so.

"You must be Samantha," she said. "I'm Rose Lambert, and I'm glad to meet you. Faith has been telling me about your ordeal and that you inquired about a room a few days ago. One of the boarders must have answered the door. They do that at times."

Faith only knew it wasn't this lady or Faith who she'd talked to. "I'm pleased to meet you, Mrs. Lambert."

"Oh we don't stand on ceremony here, child. Call me Rose."

"Yes, ma'am. . .ah, Rose. Please call me Samantha." Calling the older woman by her first name went against the way she'd been raised, but she didn't want to refuse the woman's request either. "Is there anything I can do to help?"

"Not after all you've been through today. You sit down and relax," Faith said.

Samantha took a seat at the table and smiled at Rose.

The older woman smiled back and said, "I told Faith that

you are more than welcome to share my room with me."

"Why, that is very nice of you, Rose. Thank you."

"I don't snore, or if I do, my departed husband never told me so." She grinned at Samantha.

Samantha laughed. "I don't think I do either. I certainly hope not."

"We'll settle the room situation later, but don't you worry, Samantha. You have a place to stay as long as you need it," Faith said as she basted what turned out to be two hens she was roasting. The aroma had Samantha's mouth watering, and she realized it'd been awhile since she'd eaten.

"We'll find you work, too. Only that might take a few days longer. I'm going to ask around town. I have an idea of several places that might need help," Faith continued as she slid the roaster back in the oven. She turned to Samantha with a smile. "Oh, that dress looks wonderful on you. I'm so glad it fit."

"Thank you so much for letting me borrow it. I'll take very good care of it."

"Consider it yours. I've worn it so much I'm sure my husband is getting a bit tired of it. I think I have another dress or two that will fit you. I've put on a little weight since I married, and I've noticed several outfits that are a little snug on me."

Samantha wondered if she was exaggerating a bit, but she had a feeling Faith wouldn't like it if she asked. From the way she'd treated her since she'd walked through the door, Samantha knew Faith Logan had a huge heart. "Thank you, Faith. But one more should do me until I can go to work and buy some—"

"No need to spend your money if you don't have to, I

always say," Rose said, giving her opinion on the subject as if it settled the matter.

"That's right, Rose. And really, Samantha, I'd like to share what I can."

"Then I thank you, Faith."

The sound of a door opening cut short their conversation, and Samantha wondered if Mr. Thompson had come back. Several people were talking and laughing as they got closer to the kitchen, and she figured it might be some of the boarders. She was surprised when two young people burst into the kitchen with Mr. Thompson coming in right behind them.

"Oh, that smells good, Aunt Faith," the young man said.

"My mouth began watering as soon as Papa opened the front door," the young lady said.

"Matt, Hope, please meet Miss Carter, the lady I told you about on the way here," Mr. Thompson said. "Miss Carter, these are my children."

"I'm pleased to meet you both," Samantha said. From what Mr. Thompson had told her earlier, either his wife had passed away, or they weren't living together.

"Pleased to meet you, ma'am," Hope said.

"Yes, I'm pleased, too," Matt added.

"You cleaned up real well, Miss Carter." Ben smiled from behind his daughter.

"Ben!" Faith slapped her brother on the shoulder. "What a thing to say!"

"Well—"

"It's all right, Faith. I was a sight, you must admit, what with all that smoke and ash covering me. And please, everyone, call me Samantha."

The young people looked at their papa for permission to do so. He nodded. "I suppose it's all right, since Miss—since Samantha has asked us to. Of course she must reciprocate and call us by our first names, too."

Samantha inclined her head and nodded. "All right, Ben. It's nice to meet your children."

"Thank you." He poured himself a cup of coffee and joined her at the table. "I come in most weekends to see them and eat Faith's good cooking. But come fall, I'll have them out at the farm, and then we might all come in for some of Faith's cooking. Unless Hope has learned—"

Samantha noticed the glance Hope and her aunt shared before Faith said, "Hope is a good cook. She helps us in the kitchen most days, doesn't she, Rose?"

"She does, to be sure."

"And I need to go wash up now; then I'll be right back down to help." Hope kissed her papa on the cheek and hurried out of the room.

"I'll go do my chores," Matt said. "This smells too good to stay inside with until supper time."

"I'll be out to help when I finish this coffee."

"There's no need, Papa. I can handle it."

"I'm sure you can, son."

A shadow seemed to fall over Ben's face as he watched his son leave the room. He took a swig of coffee and looked at his sister. "They're growing up on me, Faith."

"They are, Ben. But they are becoming wonderful young people. You should be proud of them."

"Oh, I am that. But I wish time didn't fly quite so fast. Where is Gabe working today? I think I'll go give him a hand."

Faith watched her brother leave and then turned back to Samantha and Rose with a sigh. "He's really not going to be happy when he finds out Hope doesn't want to spend the harvest break at the farm."

three

Samantha couldn't help but feel a little sorry for Ben Thompson. With him on a farm and his children in town, he missed a lot of their day-to-day lives. It had to be hard on all of them. She wondered about his wife but didn't feel like she should ask.

Faith sighed and shook her head. "He's seemed so lonesome the last few times he's come to town. And Matt and Hope have made friends here. Sometimes they are torn between spending time with him and doing something with a friend on a Saturday, and neither of them want to tell him."

"He needs a wife, that man does," Rose said. "I know his heart is in the land, but I think he's torn at times, too. I wish he'd found a wife here in town before he offered to farm my place, or that my farm was in a little closer."

"So do I, Rose," Faith said. "I know he misses Molly. They all do. He's totally devoted to his children, but he can't live his life only for them. They are growing up, and even if they were on the farm now, they won't be forever. They'll have their own lives to live. Besides, much as he loves them, they can't take the place of a wife, and Molly would be the first to tell him so."

Samantha felt almost like an intruder listening to the conversation. She could only assume from it that Ben's wife had passed away and was taken aback by the relief that washed over her upon learning that he wasn't estranged from his wife. How sad for them all. She wasn't sure what to say. She sipped the tea Faith set in front of her and watched her and Rose as they worked on supper. "Are you sure there isn't anything I can help you with?" she asked.

"I don't think so, but thank you, Samantha. Mrs. Warner and Mrs. Fairmont came in from shopping while you were cleaning up, and they'll be down in the parlor before long. Gabe will be coming in soon, and we'll have supper in about an hour."

Hope came back into the kitchen, and Samantha was struck by how much she looked like her father. Hope gave her a sweet smile and turned to her aunt. "I'll go set the table now, unless you need me to do something else, Aunt Faith."

"That's fine, Hope, dear. I believe we've got everything under control in here."

Hope went into what Samantha assumed was the dining room, but she was only gone for a moment before she came back to the kitchen. "Oh, I wanted to say that I'll be glad to share my room with Miss—with Samantha."

"Oh Hope, that is very nice of you. Thank you." Samantha was touched by the young girl's suggestion. "Rose offered, too. I hate to put anyone out—"

The back door opened, and Ben, another man, and Matt all came in at the same time. The way Faith's face lit up, Samantha was pretty sure the man was her husband.

"Samantha, this is my husband, Gabe Logan." Faith's words proved her right. "You can call him Gabe."

The man walked over to the table and smiled down at Samantha. "Pleased to meet you, Samantha. I'm sorry about the fire but glad you didn't get hurt. Ben told me all about it."

"Thank you. I'm very fortunate that he came by when he did."

"She didn't like me keeping her from going back into that tent, though. At least not until the top of it caved in at the center. Once that happened, it took only a few moments for the rest to be destroyed." Ben looked at her and sighed. "I don't think I've ever been so scared as when I saw her ducking into that tent before I got there. I'm thankful she got out and I got to her before she went back in. Of course I believed she was a boy at the time. I probably would have had a heart attack if I'd known she was a woman."

For the first time, Samantha realized he'd seen her running in to get what she could. And he'd hurried to keep her from doing it again, afraid he'd be too late. She let go of a shaky breath. "It would have landed on top of my head if you hadn't stopped me."

"We're certainly glad that he did," Faith said. Her husband crossed the room to be at her side, bent down, kissed her on the cheek, and put his arm around her as she continued, "Now all you have to do is decide who to room with—Rose or Hope—and then we'll work on finding you a job, Samantha."

"Rose or Hope? Why don't I give her my room?" Matt said. "I know you ladies like your privacy, and I can stay in the new apartment over the office. It's turned out pretty nice, hasn't it, Uncle Gabe?"

"It has. That's a good idea, Matt. It would give you and Ben more room when he's here, too."

Ben nodded. "You're right, it would. We can move Matt's things after supper."

"Oh, I really hate to put you all out—" Samantha began.

"Looks like your mind has been made up for you, Samantha," Faith said. "It really is a good idea. Matt's wanted to move over there for some time now, anyway. Looks like you are an answer to his prayers."

Matt grinned and bowed in Samantha's direction. "Thank you, ma'am."

Samantha couldn't help but laugh with the others. The decision had been made.

☙

After the fire, Samantha's first inclination had been to feel sorry for herself, but now she realized it was a blessing in disguise. She'd never met more caring people in her life than Ben and his family. And even the boarders at the Logan Boardinghouse were kind.

At dinner, Samantha met the Fairmonts, the Warners, and an older gentleman named Mr. Dodson, who'd replaced a Mr. Herrington after he got married.

"Mr. Herrington's new wife was eager to set up house-keeping in her own home," Faith explained. "And they hired Gabe to build them a nice little house on a lot Mr. Herrington bought from a couple who wanted to go back East. They stop by from time to time for Sunday dinner so we keep in contact."

"Well, I'm glad that little woman wanted a place of her own," Mr. Dodson said. "Otherwise I wouldn't be here now."

Samantha couldn't help but notice that Mr. Dodson kept glancing at Rose throughout the meal, and she wondered if Rose was aware of his interest. The conversation over the meal was lively, and they all welcomed her warmly. Once they found out she was going to move into Matt's room, everyone offered to help in whatever way was needed.

After dinner, Hope and Rose took over cleanup while the men helped move Matt's things over to the apartment. Mrs. Warner and Mrs. Fairmont went up to the attic and went through the things they'd brought with them but didn't need while living in a boardinghouse. They came back down with a bedcover that was a lot more feminine than the one Matt had on his bed and curtains that matched quite well. Mrs. Fairmont even brought down a silver-plated comb and brush set she'd just replaced and a few other more feminine accessories.

Evidently the apartment was pretty much furnished so the furniture in Matt's old room stayed put, but everything else that belonged to him or looked as if it belonged to a man quickly disappeared from sight. It seemed no time at all until the room had a decidedly softer feel to it.

"Oh it's lovely," Samantha said when they all stepped back to admire the transformation. The wedding ring quilt had belonged to Mrs. Warner's mother. And the lace curtains were some Mrs. Fairmont had made herself. That they were willing to let her use them—someone they'd never met until today—Samantha didn't quite know what to say. "I've never had a room this nice before. Thank you all so much. I'll take good care of everything until I can return it."

"You are welcome," Faith said, and the other ladies echoed her. "It did turn out really nice. Now I'm going down to put on a pot of coffee. I'll brew some tea, too, if you ladies would prefer that. Please come join me, if you aren't too tired."

Even if she had been tired, Samantha wouldn't have turned down the invitation. But her eyes began to burn with tears, and she felt the need of a few minutes to herself. "Thank you. I'd love that. I'll be right down."

"Take all the time you need," Faith said as she and the others left the room. Samantha could only let out a shaky breath and blink against the tears that threatened. She hadn't been shown such kindness since she'd lived with her grandmother after her parents died in a train wreck.

She gazed around the room once more. After having slept on the ground for the last few days, she found the bed more than a little welcoming. The room was a nice size, holding the bed, a wardrobe and dresser, and even a writing table and chair by the window.

Faith had hung a churchgoing dress, two skirts, and several shirtwaists in the wardrobe. She'd also put an array of personal undergarments in the drawers. Due to the kindness of these strangers, Samantha had a place to call home and clothes to wear. Now all she had to do was find work. For the first time in days, she felt hopeful about finding a respectable job.

She hurried to the bathroom the boarders shared and splashed her face with water to keep the tears at bay before she went back downstairs and joined the others in the kitchen. Mrs. Fairmont and Mrs. Warner had joined their husbands in the parlor for their tea, but Faith and her husband and Ben and his children, along with Rose, greeted her when she entered the kitchen.

"Samantha, I was afraid you might decide to call it a night. I know you must be exhausted," Faith said. "But I'm glad you took me up on my invitation. Would you like coffee or tea?"

"Tea, please." It seemed to relax her more than coffee this time of night. "I hope you like your new apartment, Matt. I can't tell you how much I appreciate your giving up your room for me."

The young man chuckled. "Please believe me, Miss

Samantha, I appreciate your taking it."

"And he means that sincerely, Samantha," Ben said. "I have to admit it's a nice apartment. It does give us a little more space when I come to town."

"But what about when you aren't here? Is it very far away for Matt to be staying by himself?" Samantha asked, a little surprised at her concern for the young man she barely knew.

"He'll be fine. It's not much more than arm's reach across the lots. There's a good lock on the door, and Matt has his own gun. He knows how to use it if he has to. But I'm going to trust the Lord that he won't ever have a need to. And of course it doesn't hurt to know that Faith and Gabe's room looks right over at the apartment."

Samantha felt better hearing that assurance. Matt was a good-sized young man, and he did seem quite mature for his age. If his father believed he'd be all right, she might as well quit worrying.

She looked around the table at the people who'd come to her aid without knowing a thing about her and knew that she'd gained more than she'd lost that day. Much more. She loved listening to them talk about some of the possibilities for finding her work and who might or might not be needing good help.

Rose and Hope began to gather up the cups, and this time Samantha didn't let Faith talk her out of helping. She dried the dishes as Rose washed and handed them to Hope to put up. "It's the least I can do after all you've done for me. I'll not be sitting and watching you all do all the work anymore."

"Guess she told you, sis," Ben said. But the look in his eyes made Samantha think he liked that she'd lent a hand to his sister.

"Guess she did," Faith said with a smile.

Once the last cup was dried, Samantha folded the towel and laid it on the washboard. "Thank you all again. I think I'll go try out that bed. I must admit I'm quite looking forward to sleeping on a mattress and not on the ground tonight. I'll see you in the morning. Good night. I—" She looked at each one, but her gaze came to rest on Ben.

He smiled and shook his head. "Enough thanks from you for one day. You are very welcome. Sleep well."

Samantha wasn't sure what else to say so she only nodded and hurried out the door and up the stairs. She'd wanted to hug each person for their complete acceptance and eagerness to help her but had held herself back. Something about Ben Thompson touched her heart—aside from the fact that he'd saved her life. Still, after her ordeal in Kansas, she didn't welcome the feeling. She'd left there thinking she'd never find a man in all the world she could trust. . . . And she had no intention of ever getting close enough to one to want to. Yet deep down inside, she knew she wanted to trust this one. Maybe already did.

When she opened the door to her room, she was again flooded with gratefulness to be able to have a place like this to stay. She readied herself for bed and pulled her worn Bible out of the saddlebag Ben had brought in earlier. It had been her mother's, and Samantha ran a hand over the cover and held it to her chest. "Thank You, Father," she whispered. "Thank You for letting Ben Thompson save my life and bring me here to his sister's place. Thank You for all the kindness I've been shown today. Please watch over this family and the boarders and bless each one for their help. In Jesus' name. Amen."

Samantha read until her eyelids started to droop. Then she turned out the light and crawled beneath the clean bed linens. She sighed as her head sank onto the pillow. Her last thought was that the Lord had turned the day from near tragedy into a huge blessing, and she thanked Him once more.

❧

Ben watched Samantha leave the room and was taken aback by the way his heart stirred in his chest. His children elicited that kind of response from him, but this feeling was entirely different, and he couldn't put a name on it. Maybe it was a normal reaction after seeing her about to run back into that tent, afraid he wouldn't get there in time to stop her.

But he had a feeling there was more to it. She certainly did clean up real nice. That slight young man he'd thought she was had turned into a lovely, shapely young woman in one afternoon. He was more than a little relieved knowing that she was safe under his sister's roof and not out in the elements by herself somewhere between Guthrie and Oklahoma City. But he wasn't any too eager to leave her in a town with more single men than—

"She'll be fine here, Ben," Gabe said. "These ladies love nothing better than to fuss over someone who needs help— although I don't think Samantha Carter will let them fuss over her long. She seems to be quite independent."

"She'd have to be, to come here by herself, live in a tent and—" Faith shuddered. "I can't even imagine doing that. Had I not been traveling with Ben and the children, I never would have come to the territory all alone."

"I'm sure she had good reason," Rose said. "Most women don't decide to pick up and leave all that is familiar to them without one. I'm so glad you came to her aid and brought her here, Ben."

"She may be independent, but I don't think she'd have been camping out by herself if she could have found a place to stay," Faith said. "But the town is full up right now. Gabe and I had been talking about renting out the apartment only a few weeks ago. I'm glad we decided not to."

"So am I," Gabe said. "But I never really entertained that idea. I decided I didn't want anyone but family in such close proximity to my business plans and files."

"Considering Matt has been wishing he could move in over there, it worked out real well for all of us. Guess my son is fast turning into a young man, and I might as well accept it." Ben glanced at his grinning son and smiled back. "But I think it's time for us to call it a night. See you all in the morning."

Faith came and kissed him on the cheek. "It's good to have you home. I truly am so thankful that you weren't hurt helping to save Samantha, and I'm glad you brought her here."

"Thanks, Faith. So am I."

They said their good nights, and he and Matt headed across the yard to Gabe's office. They climbed the outside staircase that was lit by the light they'd left on when they'd finished moving everything over. Now it seemed to welcome them in as Matt unlocked the door and they went inside.

Gabe had planned the apartment well, and Ben was pretty sure he'd had him and Matt in mind when he drew up the plans. It was made up of two rooms and a bathroom. The bedroom was a nice size, and the parlor/kitchen area was even nicer. A small, round table and two chairs stood in front of the window overlooking the yard between it and at the boardinghouse. Ben couldn't help but notice the light on in what had been Matt's room. Samantha was probably still too keyed up after the day she'd had to sleep. He could well understand. Tired as he was, he still felt wound up himself, and he let Matt have first dibs on the bathroom while he familiarized himself with the kitchen area.

A small cookstove would help to keep the apartment warm in the winter. With the boardinghouse right there, the stove might not be used to cook much, but it was nice to have if the weather was bad and one couldn't get out. Faith had even stocked coffee, tea, cocoa, and sugar. Ben smiled remembering Faith as a child. He was the one who'd taught her to make hot chocolate. He couldn't ask for a better sister. And she was still there for him and his children, even as she was adjusting to being a married woman again.

When they'd both come out here a little over a year ago, he and Faith were both widowed. But it didn't take long for her to find Gabe—or rather for them to find each other. It took a little longer for Gabe to convince her that he loved her enough to accept the fact that they might never have children. They seemed happier every time he saw them, and for that he was extremely thankful—and more than a little envious.

Ben sighed and bent his head in prayer. *Lord, please forgive me. I know it's wrong to be jealous of what my sister and Gabe have. But I sure miss being married and having someone to share my life with. Someone to see the sunrise with each morning and share my awe of You and the beauty You created. Someone to share the good times and even the bad. Please help me to be satisfied with the life You've given me, Lord. I know I'm blessed. Molly was a wonderful wife, and she gave me two great children. Please help me to count my blessings instead of longing for more. In Jesus' name. Amen.*

"Papa, you all right?"

Ben raised his head to see his son leaning against the doorframe leading into the bedroom. He smiled. "I'm fine, son. Just talking to the Lord for a bit."

His son nodded. "I've been doing some of that, too. I sure am glad you weren't hurt saving Miss Samantha today. She seems nice."

"She does."

"And she's real pretty."

"She is." That was an understatement if ever he'd given one.

"You're a man of few words tonight, Papa."

"I am." Ben chuckled. "Guess I'm tired, son. You are right. Sam seems to be a very nice woman, and she's real easy on the eyes, too."

"Sam?"

"That's what she first introduced herself as, and the name kind of stuck with me. But she doesn't look like a Sam now."

His son grinned at him. "No, she sure doesn't. Maybe you ought to think about courting her."

Ben sighed. The idea had crossed his mind a time or two before it had tried to settle in. But he'd chased it right back out. He'd only met the woman today. "Son, keep in mind that we don't know a lot about her. . . ."

Ben didn't like the direction his thoughts were taking him. He didn't want to doubt that Samantha was everything she appeared to be. But he'd lived enough life to know that first impressions weren't always correct.

"Well," Matt said, "that only means you need to get to know her better. That's the only way you'll find out if she's the kind of woman we think she is."

Ben was a little surprised at his son's suggestion. He'd feared his children might resent it if he ever did find a woman he wanted to marry. Instead his son seemed to be prodding him to do exactly that. Matt truly was growing up faster by the day.

four

Ben had been glad to put a pot of coffee on when he woke up the next morning. These city folk let themselves sleep a little longer before they started their day. He'd already poured his second cup and been out on the small porch, enjoying the sunrise and seeing the neighborhood come awake, when Gabe came out of the boardinghouse. Ben wasn't surprised when Gabe waved and headed over toward the apartment—he'd halfway been expecting him.

"Come on in. I'll pour you a cup of coffee. Faith stocked us up on that real well. Did you come to see how we liked our first night in this fine apartment you built, or is it something more along the lines of what I've been thinking we should do?"

Gabe accepted the cup of coffee and took a sip before answering. "I knew you'd like it here, so I guess I came for the second reason—if it's the same as mine."

"With Samantha under your roof, we need to find out why she left Kansas or at the very least if she is wanted for anything." Ben hated putting his thoughts into words, but there they were.

"That's right. I think that little woman is just what she seems to be, but one has to think that if she made the trip here by herself and was camping out, she could be on the run from something or someone. I want to make sure it's not a crime of some sort, although I can't believe it is."

"Neither can I, but you're right. We need to make sure."

Matt came into the room right then. "Can I have a cup of that coffee, Papa?"

"Sure." He poured his son a cup and handed it to him. "Gabe and I have something to take care of—"

"I heard. And I understand why you think you should find out what you can. But I don't think Miss Samantha is running from the law."

"Neither do we, Matt. But it'll put our minds at rest to make sure."

Matt nodded and took a sip from his cup.

"We won't be long. If you want, you can go on over to the boardinghouse for breakfast," Ben told his son, who was nearly as tall as he was now.

"Nah. I'll wait until you get back. That way I won't have to answer any questions about where you are."

Gabe chuckled. "Good thinking, Matt. You know those women well."

"Yeah, I do, Uncle Gabe. And Papa—once you find out she's not running from the law, are you gonna think about courting her?"

Gabe laughed as Ben shook his head and grinned.

"I might give it some thought, son."

"Good. That's all I wanted to know. See you in a bit."

Ben and Gabe each took one last swig of their coffee and headed out the door. But it wasn't until they reached the bottom step that Gabe said, "You thinking of courting our new boarder, are you?"

Ben shrugged. "The thought may have crossed my mind. And it crossed Matt's that I should. He brought it up last night."

"Well, if she's what she seems, I'd say you could sure do worse. She's nice to look at, and you know there aren't a lot of single women to choose from in these parts."

"That's for sure."

Some stores were just opening up as they reached the center of town, but traffic wasn't bad yet. They made their way to the marshal's office, and if he was surprised to see the two of them that early in the morning, he didn't say so. "Mornin', Gabe, Ben. What can I do for you two?"

It didn't take long to let him know their concerns, and Ben was glad it was Gabe, not him, telling the marshal that they wanted to check out Samantha Carter.

"I'll get right on it," the marshal said. "If she's running from anything, more than likely it's from a man or family problems of some kind. But could be she wanted a new start somewhere like a lot of us did."

That was certainly the scenario Ben hoped for. He didn't like the idea that she might be running from some man one bit.

The marshal looked through his records and wanted posters and quickly came up with nothing on Samantha Carter. "I'll wire Kansas and see if there is anything new we haven't received yet. It shouldn't take long to find out if they have anything on her. I'll get back to you soon as I find out anything. In the meantime, figure that no news is good news."

Ben let out an inward sigh of relief. Surely if she'd committed any kind of crime, the marshal would already have something on it. He sent up a silent prayer that she was simply a woman wanting to make a new start—and that nothing any different turned up.

Samantha was up and dressed early. She'd slept better than she had in weeks, and she was determined to get downstairs early enough to help Faith with breakfast. That seemed the least she could do after all Faith's family had done for her. She slipped out of her room, and the boardinghouse was so quiet she hoped she might be the first down, until the smell of fresh coffee and bacon wafted up the stairs. She hurried down to find Faith rolling out biscuits while Rose fried bacon in a huge cast-iron skillet.

"Good morning! What can I do to help? And please don't say I can't." She smiled at both women.

Faith chuckled. "Well, let's see. Why don't you crack those eggs there into a bowl for me?" She nodded toward the counter where a large wire basket sat filled with eggs. "We'll scramble them up with some peppers and onions. The boarders really like them that way."

"I'll be glad to." Samantha took the apron Rose grabbed out of a drawer and put it over her neck, tying it around her waist. She quickly went to work on the eggs and only managed to get a couple of pieces of shell in the bowl. She quickly dug them out with a spoon and asked, "What next?"

Faith handed her a whisk and a small bowl filled with chopped onions and bell peppers. "Beat them up a little, and then add the onions and bell pepper and stir some more."

"I should be able to manage that."

"I'm sure you can."

Samantha grinned as she went about the business of whisking the eggs. "I love scrambled eggs—omelets, too." Being in this kitchen brought back sweet memories of helping her mother before she passed away and then being taught by her grandmother. But once she was on her own and living in boardinghouses, she hadn't had the opportunity to cook. It appeared she'd forgotten most of what she'd learned.

"So do I," Faith agreed. "And it's much quicker and easier than frying them singly. I forgot to tell you that breakfast is from seven until nine. I set it out on the sideboard in the dining room, and everyone eats when they want to within that time frame. I serve a light lunch at noon the same way, on the sideboard. And we all eat dinner together as we did last night. For breakfast or lunch, you are welcome to eat in the dining room or bring your plate back in here and eat with us."

"Thank you, Faith. You certainly provide a lot for your boarders, and I really need to pay you in advance. I have enough money for a month or two. Surely I'll find work by then."

"No, you wait to pay me until you have a job. You'll find something. I'm sure of it." Faith took the large bowl of beaten eggs from Samantha and poured them into the skillet she'd melted some butter in.

"I'm feeling much more hopeful than I was a few days ago. After breakfast I'll go out and start looking again."

"There really isn't any hurry, Samantha. Why don't you let yourself get used to the town and think about places you might want to work. In the meantime, I'll do some asking around and see if any of my friends can come up with anything. Tomorrow is the Lord's Day. Monday is soon enough to start applying unless we come up with something great before then."

"With all the preparations for the territorial celebration

next week, I'm afraid all I'll be able to find is something temporary. But I suppose that would be better than nothing."

"You never know. There are bound to be some openings in the classifieds." Faith used a fork to scramble the egg mixture, and in what seemed no time at all, those eggs were fluffy and ready to eat. She put them into a chafing dish and asked Samantha to take them to the dining room. Rose took the crisp bacon in and showed her where to place the dish over the hot water to keep the eggs warm until the boarders served themselves.

They went back to the kitchen where Faith was pulling the biscuits out of the oven. Samantha's mouth began to water.

Laughter coming from the hall alerted them that some of the boarders had made their way down to the dining room.

"It's probably the men. Their wives usually eat a bit later," Faith said as she took the biscuits into them and came back to the kitchen at the same time her husband came in from outside and dropped a kiss on her cheek.

Samantha assumed Faith's husband had been over talking to Ben or checking on things in his office.

"I had some errands to run. It's a beautiful day out," Gabe turned to Samantha. "Good morning. Did you sleep well?"

"I slept wonderful, thank you." The house, the people had all been so welcoming; she hadn't felt so safe and secure in years.

Ben and Matt came in then, and Samantha caught her breath at the smile Ben sent her way. He was a very good-looking man, with reddish-brown hair and green eyes. And he looked as if he'd slept well, too. He handed her a newspaper. "Matt and I went to get one fresh off the press.

Maybe there will be something new in the classifieds this morning."

Samantha wasn't prepared for the spark of electricity that shot up her arm and straight to her heart at the touch of their fingertips. "Thank you—we were talking about looking in the paper earlier. I'll go over the classifieds after breakfast."

They all went into the dining room, where the gentlemen she'd met the night before were discussing the upcoming territorial events, and Samantha found herself looking forward to seeing the new governor installed.

The men filled their plates first, and then Faith insisted that Samantha fill hers next. She helped herself to some of those fluffy eggs, bacon, and a hot biscuit, and then headed back to the kitchen.

"You really need to get the lay of the city down before you take off looking for work," Faith said. "There are some areas—"

"You might not want to try to find work in, and they don't always advertise exactly what kind of position they are hiring for," Rose said bluntly.

"Oh, I do know that. I found myself over there the other day and quickly retreated once I figured things out."

"How much of Guthrie have you actually seen?" Ben asked as he poured himself a cup of coffee.

"Not much. It rained the day I came in, so I pitched my tent outside of town and then came in the next day. That's when I wound up over by—" Hope appeared in the doorway with her plate, and Samantha got the message when Ben cleared his throat. She didn't want to say exactly where she'd wound up in front of Hope either. "Good morning, Hope."

"Good morning!" Hope took a seat beside her father.

"Anyway, I looked down Division Street and only saw one help-wanted sign," Samantha continued, "but it was for a barber. The next day I came in, but I was looking for a place to stay and had no luck at all. I didn't want to live in a tent forever. I was debating on whether or not to go on to Oklahoma City and try to find a place to stay until I could find a job."

"Well I'm glad you didn't get that far," Faith said. "You'll find something here—I'm sure of it."

Samantha hoped so. She'd hate to leave this house and these people after they'd been so kind to her. Somehow she didn't feel quite so alone now. She bowed her head as Gabe said a blessing. Samantha silently added her own prayer before taking her first bite. *Thank You, Lord, for letting Ben find me and for leading me here. Thank You for always being faithful to look after me. Please help me to find work soon so I can stay right here. In Jesus' name, I pray. Amen.*

❧

Ben waited until Samantha raised her head. "I'll be glad to show you the lay of the land today," he said. "I'm sure Hope and Matt would be glad to tag along unless they have something else planned."

"Actually, Papa, Mindy Ellis asked if I could come help her decide what dress to wear to the ceremony next week. I promise I won't be gone all that long, and I'm sure to be back by the time you get through showing Samantha around."

"What about your chores?"

"I'll do them all before I go and be back in plenty of time to help Aunt Faith with dinner."

Ben nodded. He knew she'd keep her word. "All right. You may go."

Hope jumped up and kissed her father on the cheek. "Thank you, Papa! I'll go get started on my chores now."

"What about breakfast?"

"I'm done." She grabbed her plate and took it to the sink, quickly washed it and put it on the drainboard, then hurried out of the kitchen.

"What about you, Matt? Do you have any plans for today?"

"Well, I'd kind of like to go help with the Beadle place. They're putting in the staircase today. But I don't have to if—"

"No, it's all right. You go on and help out there."

"Thanks, Papa!" Matt quickly finished his breakfast and followed Hope's example, washing his own plate and cup before hurrying outside.

While no one had mentioned anything, Ben was aware his son liked building as much as he liked farming. And he supposed it was good Matt had a chance to learn both at this age. He'd have to make a decision one of these days on what it was he really wanted to do, but all Ben wanted was for him to be happy at whatever it was he chose.

But today Ben wondered if his son was trying to matchmake by making sure he and Samantha had some time to themselves. After all, Matt was the one who'd suggested that Ben court Samantha. Well, he wasn't going to complain. It would be easier to show her around town without their every move being watched by his children.

Besides, Faith had mentioned once that Hope and Matt sometimes turned down invitations from friends because he'd be in town. Maybe now they'd feel as if they could tell him they'd like to do something with their friends on the weekends. "You'd think they were afraid I was going to change my mind." Ben looked down at his nearly full plate of food and wondered how they could both be finished so quickly. "Let's finish breakfast. Then you can look over that paper and see where you might want to try, Samantha. It might be best to wait until Monday, though, to actually apply for anything. It gets real busy in town on Saturdays."

"I told her that, too, Ben," Faith said.

"So will you let me show you the town, Sam? Ah, I mean, Samantha?" He bit his bottom lip and gave her a grin. He was relieved when she smiled back.

"I'd be glad to take you up on your offer, Ben. I'll help Faith clean up, and then we can be on our way, unless you have things you need to do first?"

"You helped with breakfast. No need to do dishes," Faith said.

"That's true," Rose added. "I might start to feel unneeded."

"Oh, I wouldn't want that," Samantha said. "I'm sorry. I didn't mean—"

"Oh no, don't think you've done anything wrong. I was only teasing, Samantha," Rose said.

"She was," Faith assured her. "We're thankful for the help, but I don't want you thinking you have to lend a hand with everything around here. Especially not when you are trying to find a job. Besides, I'll feel better if you know your way around Guthrie. There are a lot of men in this town, and while most of them treat women with respect, there are always some who don't."

"Yes, I know. And I appreciate that you have my best interests at heart. I'm glad to have Ben show me the lay of the land, so to speak, but I do know how to take care of myself, I promise. I don't want you worrying about me every time I leave the house."

"Oh we won't," Faith said. "Not once we are sure you know your way around."

"She'll have a good idea about that by the time we get back." And Ben wasn't leaving for the farm tomorrow unless she did. Suddenly it became of utmost importance to him that Samantha Carter really know her way around this city.

five

Ben felt quite proud to have Samantha's hand rest lightly on his arm as they took off down Noble Street toward Division. He was glad she hadn't been upset when he called her Sam. Somehow that's the first name he wanted to call her, no matter how womanly she looked.

"What was it like the day you arrived here?" she asked, looking up at him with those big blue eyes.

"When we got here, most of the city lots were taken. Gabe and I kept going up and down streets until we found some empty ones to lay claim to. But it's worked out well. We aren't right in the heart of the city, but it's much better suited for a boardinghouse than downtown would have been."

"I can see how it would be," Samantha said as they turned right on Division and headed toward the center of town.

The traffic was already picking up, with wagons and people on horseback heading to work or coming in for supplies. Guthrie was to be the territorial capital, after all, and many people came in from their farms and ranches to do business on the weekends. All the restaurants were busy, and people were going in and out of the many shops in town.

Samantha looked from one side of the street to the other. "With the rain and all, and not knowing my way around, I didn't realize Guthrie was actually this large a town. One would think it had been here for years."

Ben chuckled. "It was a mess a year ago. Oh, the vision for

the city was pretty good, but the reality wasn't so good those first days. People laid claims all over the place, and fighting broke out over many of them. But once they got settlers off the streets, it all began to make sense. And they moved fast to put all the planned improvements in place. What they didn't plan well for was the governing part of it. But it came together pretty fast once they got the right people in office."

"I'm sure it was exciting to be here at the beginning, though."

"Oh it was. But things have settled down a lot, and it's turning into a nice town." It could use a few more single women, though. Ben would have had to be blind to have missed the admiring looks Samantha had received from one man after another as they walked down the street. She did look quite pretty this morning. She had on a dark-blue skirt and crisp white blouse, and her hair was put up in a very becoming style. He still couldn't believe this woman had looked like a young man only yesterday.

But as he caught the glance of one more man settle on her, he was glad she had been dressed as a male when she first arrived in the area. The thought of some unsavory character coming up on her in that tent all alone made him shudder.

By the time they reached Harrison, they had to dodge traffic as they crossed the street. A help-wanted sign sat in the window of a laundry, and Samantha headed for it, but Ben stopped her from entering. "That is really hard work, day in and day out, Samantha. Why don't you see what else you can find? And besides, what about the openings you found in the paper? Don't you want to check them out first?"

"I suppose I should. I'm just eager to find work. Faith won't take any money from me until I do, and I—"

"You'll find a job. Don't feel you have to settle for the first thing you find. I'm sure you are well qualified for many other positions that might be a little easier on you."

"Perhaps." She smiled at him, and Ben's chest tightened. Something about this woman made him want to reassure her, to protect her and—and he really didn't know anything about her except that she had the prettiest blue eyes he'd ever seen and her smile somehow made his day brighter.

"What was it you did up in Kansas?" Maybe she'd open up about why she'd come here on her own.

Samantha hesitated a moment and managed to avoid his question as she pointed at a help-wanted sign down the street aways. "Look—isn't that one of the places that was in the paper?"

Obviously she wasn't in a mood to confide in him. "Yes, you'd mentioned that Jeffery & Wright Grocery needed a clerk. Let's go see if they still do."

"Then there is the law office of L. L. Johnson on Harrison near the grocer's. Which one should I look into first?"

Ben's first thought was the law office because it would be an easier position and she wouldn't have to stand on her feet all day, but then he realized she might be alone in the office with some man and—

He needed to get a grip on himself. He'd barely met this woman, and here he was, worried about her being alone with some other man. "Either one is fine. Which one do you think you'd like to try first?"

"Let's go with the one we come across first," Samantha said.

The law office turned out to be on the other side of the street and the grocer's on the same side they were on, so they stopped in there first. The manager assumed that Ben was applying for the position, but once he found out it was Samantha, he began to shake his head. "I'm sorry, miss, but there's a lot of heavy lifting with this job. I'm lookin' for a strong man for the position."

"I understand," Samantha said with a sigh. "Thank you for your time."

They walked outside, and Ben said, "This job could have turned out to be as hard as working at the laundry, Samantha. I think I'm glad you didn't get it."

"Well, I'm not sure how I feel, but there's nothing I can do about it. Let's go try the lawyer's office."

They crossed the street, again dodging freight wagons, farm wagons, and carriages of all sizes. When they entered the office, a woman at the front desk looked up, and Ben wondered if perhaps they'd already filled the position.

"Hello," Samantha said. "I'm here about the position that was in the paper for a receptionist. Has it been filled yet?"

The older woman looked Samantha up and down. "No. Not yet, but you aren't what we are looking for."

"Might I ask what or who it is that you are looking for?"

The woman looked over her glasses. "For starters, someone not quite so young and pretty. I'll not have my husband working with you, my dear. I'll keep working here until we find someone not near as attractive as you or until a man applies."

Ben noticed the color that crept up Samantha's cheeks as she inhaled sharply. "I can assure you that I am not after a married man. . .Mrs. Johnson, I presume? In fact, I'm not after a man at all. I only want work."

"Please don't take this as an insult to you, dear. A high compliment instead. And realize that I know my husband quite well. I wish you luck in finding employment."

"Thank you," Samantha said, resignation in her voice. "I wish you the best in finding the right person."

Ben was impressed with how Samantha squared her shoulders and turned to leave without a backward glance. But once they got outside the office, she turned to him.

"How sad for her that she can't trust her husband. I guess I always assumed that once a person was married they stayed in love and didn't stray. At least that's how it was with my parents and grandparents until the day they died. But I've found that isn't true for many, and it breaks my heart."

"It is sad." Ben nodded. He agreed with her view of marriage, but he wasn't sure what to say next. The statement she'd made about not being after a man at all had him wondering why and thinking she might have been disillusioned somewhere along the way. At any rate, it didn't encourage him to bring up the subject of courting. At least not now. And what was he thinking, anyway? He still really knew nothing about her except that she had no family, she'd left Kansas, she needed a job, and she wasn't looking for a man. That wasn't nearly enough information to be able to conclude that they'd be right for each other.

❧

Samantha and Ben next tried a drugstore that had advertised for help. But the position had been filled by the time they arrived, and she was beginning to lose her optimism.

"Don't get discouraged, Samantha. Think of it this way—did you really want to do heavy lifting at the grocery store all day? And I don't think you are the kind of woman who would want to be chased around your desk by a married man."

"You're right. But what about the drugstore? That job wouldn't have been hard, and other people worked there—"

"Oh but you didn't get turned down there. The position was already filled. You can't count it." He smiled.

Samantha laughed outright. "Okay. I won't count it. I could try the laundry—"

"Sam, do you really want to do laundry all day? I'd think all that heat and steam would take the curl right out of your hair." That earned him a small chuckle. "Come on. Cheer up. I'll buy you some lunch."

She sighed and nodded. "All right, I will take you up on your offer provided that you let me buy you lunch when I do get a job."

He heaved an exaggerated sigh and said, "Agreed. And you will get one."

Samantha took the arm he proffered, and they headed down the street. She had to admit that being accompanied by Ben Thompson made the rejections not quite so bitter as they might have been if she were alone. He had such an encouraging nature that it was hard not to feel better.

He took her to Miller's Restaurant, where he said he knew the proprietors, and true enough, they greeted him as a long-lost friend and gave them a nice table by a window.

"We don't see much of you when you come to town, Ben. Guess that sister of yours feeds you real good over at the boardinghouse."

"That she does, Mrs. Miller."

"And who is this lovely young woman you've brought with you?" Mrs. Miller nodded in Samantha's direction. She could feel her face flush as the older woman appraised her.

"This is Miss Samantha Carter, who is staying at the

boardinghouse. She's looking for work in Guthrie."

Mrs. Miller's eyebrow lifted. "Oh? What kind of work are you looking for, Miss Carter?"

"Well, after seeing how few positions are available right now, I'll take about any respectable job. We inquired at the grocer's, but he wanted a man. And we tried at a law office, but I think they'd be happier with a man, too—"

"She was a little too attractive in the wife's opinion."

Mrs. Miller threw back her head and laughed. "I can see where she might be, but that certainly wouldn't hurt her chances here."

"Here?"

Samantha looked around just as Ben did. The place was very busy, and she could see how Mrs. Miller might need help.

"Look around you, Ben. I can't keep good help, and I could sure use another waitress or two, especially with all the people coming to town next week for the celebrations. I can always use more help here. Most of the single women marry pretty quickly out here, and their husbands don't want them working around all these men, so turnover is very high here in Guthrie."

"You really need help?" Samantha said.

"I do. Have you ever waited tables before?"

Samantha shook her head. "No. But I learn quickly."

"When could you start?"

"Wait!" Ben said. "It'd be about as hard to work here as it would at the laundry or the grocer's, either one, Samantha. You'll be on your feet all day. Are you sure—?"

"I'm quite sure, Ben. I need work, and Mrs. Miller needs help." She looked up at the woman with a smile. "When do you want me to start?"

Mrs. Miller looked from her to Ben and back again. "I could use you now—"

"Mrs. Miller, she only arrived yesterday, and tomorrow is Sunday—"

The proprietor grinned and looked back at Samantha. "How about you start on Monday? Can you be here by eight in the morning?"

"I can. I'll be glad to start on Monday. Thank you!"

"You're welcome. Wear a skirt and white shirtwaist, similar to what you have on, and I'll provide an apron. Now, what can I get the two of you? I recommend the chicken potpie."

"That will be fine with me." Samantha settled back in her chair, trying to take in the fact that she actually had found work.

"I'll take that, too."

"I'll have it out right away," Mrs. Miller said as she turned away.

Ben didn't look too happy when she left the table. "I really wish you'd have waited a few days before taking this waitress position, Samantha. Like she said, she always needs help. You could be passing up a really good position you haven't even seen yet."

He really did seem upset. Samantha truly believed he had her best interests at heart, but she had to have work and the sooner the better, the way she looked at it. At this point, she was thankful that Mrs. Miller hadn't asked her what her last position had been. It'd been all she could do to avoid answering Ben when he'd asked what she did in Kansas. If he knew that she'd been a teacher, he would be even more upset at her taking this job. But the semester was just starting and there wouldn't be any need for a new teacher right now. And she wasn't sure—

"Don't you think you could put her off a few days and. . ."

It was only when Ben continued that she realized she hadn't said anything to put his mind at ease. "That wouldn't be right, Ben. I've already told her I'd take the job. Mrs. Miller seems a very nice woman, and if another position came along, I'm sure she would wish me well."

He sat back in his chair and sighed. "You're right. She would. And she'll be good to you. Besides, it really is your decision to make."

"Thank you. I do appreciate your concern for me." And she did. But she didn't want him feeling responsible for her just because he'd rescued her the other day. He certainly didn't owe her anything. She was the one who owed him her very life.

➤

Ben tried to hide his frustration, but it wasn't easy to do. He didn't like the idea of Samantha working here. It wasn't that the Millers wouldn't be good employers—they would. And it wasn't that he didn't think she was up to the job—she was.

It was more that every man in the place had been finding it hard to keep their eyes off her, and he was finding it every bit as difficult to hide how he felt about that. He'd glared at more than one of them already. But Samantha seemed oblivious to the admiring looks she was getting.

"I don't want you working any harder than you have to, and I feel sure you could find something else." He nodded toward a waitress who was balancing a large tray full of filled dishes above her head. "Those trays can get pretty heavy."

"I'm not a weakling, Ben."

"I know. I just. . ." He wanted to tell her that she couldn't work there, but he didn't have that right.

"And I won't stop looking, Ben. But I don't want to turn down a job I know I can do. Please understand. Besides—"

"I know. It is really none of my business." And it wasn't. But deep down, he kind of wanted it to be.

"You saved my life, Ben Thompson. I'm not about to tell you to mind your own business. But I will tell you that if it gets to be too much, I'll quit. How's that?"

Her expression was so earnest Ben had to smile at her. "I suppose it will have to do."

Mrs. Miller brought out their potpies and waited until they'd both had a bite. "How is it?"

"It's wonderful," Samantha said.

"It's exactly like I remembered, Mrs. Miller," Ben said.

"Good. Enjoy. And I'll see you on Monday morning, Miss Carter. . .or maybe at church tomorrow. Good day." She left a ticket on the table and went back to work.

They enjoyed their meal in silence for a few moments, and then Ben said, "Well, since you have a job, I suppose we can spend the afternoon showing you the rest of the town and how to get from the boardinghouse to wherever you want to go."

"I'd like that. Thank you."

Ben didn't know if she was thanking him for offering to show her around more or for dropping the subject of the waitressing job. But as he looked into her blue eyes, it suddenly didn't matter. "You're welcome."

He'd have to trust the Lord to look after her, because it was obvious that Samantha Carter had a mind of her own.

six

On Sunday, Samantha was more than happy to attend church with the Thompsons, the Logans, Rose, and several others from the boardinghouse. They'd all celebrated her finding a job the night before, and Samantha was beginning to believe she'd made the right decision in coming to Guthrie. As she sat between Faith and Ben on a pew near the middle of church and let the peace of simply being there sink in, Samantha began to relax. The tension between her and the principal of the school she'd taught at had grown over the time. She'd been able to ignore his unseemly remarks and avoid his unwanted advances toward her for months, but the last straw broke the day he'd actually tried to corner her in her classroom and threatened that if she didn't give in to his advances, he'd ruin her reputation anyway.

As the principal advanced, the Lord must have been watching over her, for He sent her best friend and another teacher, Annie Rogers, to knock on the classroom door and enter the room. The timing was perfect—Annie entered right before Samantha had to defend herself with the small gavel she'd grabbed from her desk and hidden behind her back. Samantha had given notice right then and there.

That very night, with Annie's help, Samantha had packed the few personal items she had at the boardinghouse, told her landlady she was leaving, and caught the next train headed south. She had no doubt that Mr. Jackson would paint her in a bad light whether she stayed or went, and even if her friend took up for her, she had her own job and reputation to think of. Samantha could only pray that the principal wouldn't give Annie any trouble over what she'd seen.

But now, for the first time in a long time, Samantha felt she could breathe easy. Well, except for sometimes when she caught Ben looking at her. Then she seemed to get a catch in her breath while her heart did a funny little twist. She was attracted to the man despite her best intentions never to let herself begin to care about any man—ever.

After the episode with her principal, who was married to a wonderful woman, and then the lawyer's wife who couldn't trust her husband with a young woman working in his office, Samantha was more than a little determined never to let herself fall in love.

Yet as she stood to sing the first hymn of the morning and found herself sharing a hymnal with Ben Thompson, bringing them into closer contact, she couldn't ignore the way her heart did a now familiar little flip and dive toward her stomach. *Dear Lord, please help me to concentrate on You during this service and not the man beside me. Help me to be thankful for him and his family, but keep me from. . .caring too much about Ben Thompson. You know what's needed, Lord. Please help me only to concentrate on You.*

She sighed as peace stole over her when she finished her silent prayer, and she was able to sing with all her heart and give her attention to the prayer and the sermon that followed. The sermon was taken from 1 Thessalonians and focused on being joyful always, praying continually, and giving thanks in all circumstances. She loved that verse. Oh, it was good to be back in church with other believers, and it felt wonderful to be sitting on a pew full of people who cared enough to take her in when they knew nothing about her. She had much to be thankful for—including the man beside her. Without him, she might not be here today. She only had to protect her heart from caring too much about Ben Thompson.

≈

Ben couldn't bring himself to leave first thing Monday morning as usual. There was no way he was going to head back to the farm until he saw Samantha safely to work. And he really didn't want to leave then.

But he couldn't stay in Guthrie—he had the responsibility of farming Rose's land, which he thought of as his own place. He'd planned on talking to her about buying her out finally, but with all that had happened with Samantha and moving Matt and all, he hadn't had a chance to do it. But he wasn't worried about it right now. Rose wasn't going to pull the farm out from under him, and there was no real hurry. Still, he had to get back to it. He'd told Homer he'd be back by today, and he would—a little later than usual.

He was taking a last drink of coffee and was about to leave the apartment and head to the boardinghouse when his son came out of his room.

"You leaving this morning, Papa?"

"Sometime—I'm not sure when, though. I want to make sure Samantha knows her way to work first. And I wanted to see if you will make sure she gets home safely when she gets off work."

"I'll be glad to. Do you know what time that will be?"

"No."

"Then how can I—"

"Go by Miller's Restaurant on your way home from school and check and see."

Matt nodded. "All right. That'll be no problem. Is something bothering you, Papa?"

How did he tell his son that Samantha Carter bothered him? That he couldn't get her out of his mind and that he didn't want her working at a restaurant where single men came to eat off and on all day long? That he was afraid she might be taken when he came back to town. And that he still wasn't sure about anything concerning her. They hadn't heard back from the marshal yet and—

"Papa?"

"I'm fine, son. Just got a lot on my mind." At least that was true. "Let's go get some breakfast. Your aunt Faith ought to have it out by now."

"I don't need any nudging. I'm starving. Let's go," Matt said, hurrying out the door.

Ben sent up a silent prayer thanking the good Lord for his children. If Matt sensed that he was in a quandary, he didn't say so, nor did he ask any questions. He was a great son, and Hope was a wonderful daughter. Ben hadn't spent as much time with either of them as he would have liked this past weekend, yet they seemed quite happy with the time they'd had.

From all reports, they'd both had a good day Saturday— Hope with her friend and Matt helping with the Beadle place. Maybe he'd encourage them to spend some time doing what they wanted on Saturdays from now on. It'd only be fair, as he hoped to be able to spend some with Samantha. He only hoped it wasn't all at Miller's Restaurant, making sure some guy didn't claim her.

They opened the back door and went into Faith's kitchen

where the aroma of ham and fried potatoes surrounded them. Ben loved the smell of his sister's cooking. Their mother had taught her all she knew, and Faith's meals sometimes took him back to wonderful childhood memories. Right now the aromas in her kitchen made his stomach grumble.

Matt headed straight into the dining room to fill a plate, right as Gabe came back into the kitchen, his own plate loaded with food. Rose followed Matt, but Samantha was nowhere in sight. Ben turned to his sister, who held out a fresh cup of coffee to him.

"Thanks, sis. Has Samantha come down yet?"

"Yes, she has. She came down to get a cup of coffee and take it back to her room so she could finish getting ready for work. She should be back down anytime now."

"Good. I want to make sure she remembers the way to the restaurant. Thought I'd walk downtown with her."

Faith didn't look at him, but he caught her smile. "That sounds like a good idea to me. But you know we drove by there again yesterday on our way home from church."

"I know."

Faith nodded. "Still, it's always a good idea to make sure one knows where one is going."

"That's what I thought."

"Well, grab yourself a plate. You might have time to make a dent in it before she gets back downstairs."

Ben rubbed his jaw and grinned. "Think I'll do that."

Hope came in from the dining room right then, and he dropped a kiss on the top of her head. "Morning, sunshine."

"Good morning, Papa."

Ben continued into the dining room, but he'd no more than filled his plate and come back to take a seat beside his daughter when Samantha came into the kitchen. She looked mighty fine, dressed in a different skirt and blouse than he'd seen before and a blue bow holding up her curls. She smiled, and his heart warmed at the sight of her.

"Good morning, everyone," Samantha said. "I must admit to being a little nervous today. Please say a prayer that I don't drop one of those loaded trays today—or any day, for that matter."

"You'll do fine," Rose said. "Remember to balance like you did last night."

Last night? What had happened that he didn't know about?

His sister must have caught his quizzical look because she said, "After you and Matt went to the apartment last night, Samantha voiced her concern over carrying those big trays at the restaurant, so we did some practice runs."

"Oh, I would have loved to have seen that," Matt said.

"So would've I," Ben said. "How'd it go?"

Samantha chuckled. "Didn't go so great at first. I had things sliding all over the place. Thankfully, the dishes were empty at first."

"She got better, though," Faith said. "You'll do fine today. I don't doubt it for a moment."

"I hope so." Samantha turned to him. "I'm glad I got to see you before you left today, Ben. I really can't thank you enough—"

"Samantha, we've already had this conversation. Besides, I haven't left yet. I'm going to make sure you know your way to the restaurant before I leave."

"I think I do. There's no need to take up part of your day—"

"I think you do, too, but we'll all feel better *knowing* you do." Ben grinned, pushed back from the table, and stood.

"Well, all right, but your breakfast is going to get cold."

Faith grabbed his plate and shook her head. "No, it won't. I'll keep it warm for him. And he's right, Samantha. We'll all feel better knowing you know your way there and back."

"Everyone's concern means more to me than I can say." She looked up at Ben. "I'm ready to go, if you are."

He was ready to see her to the restaurant. But he wasn't too happy about having to leave her there. "Let's go."

❧

Samantha was glad Ben hadn't left without saying good-bye, but she wished he didn't feel he had to watch over her every minute. He'd done more than most men ever would by keeping her out of her burning tent that day—he certainly owed her nothing else. But she owed him.

She stopped in the street and turned to him. "Ben, I really don't want to take up all your time. You have a farm to work and all kinds of chores to do, I'm sure. I do know my way to the restaurant, and I hate to be a burden to you."

"You couldn't be a burden to anyone, Samantha. I only want to put my mind—and everyone else's in my family—to rest so we're all confident that you know your way."

"You know, if I got lost, I could stop and ask someone for directions."

"I'm certain you could. But please, indulge me at this?"

After all he'd done for her, now he was asking her for something, and she wasn't about to turn him down. She gave in and took the arm he offered. "All right. I suppose that is the least I can do."

As they walked along, she read out the street names and

told him which way to turn at each one until they ended up right outside the restaurant about five minutes early.

"See? I did know my way here." She grinned up at him.

"You did. And that relieved my mind greatly. I guess I'd better let you get in there to work."

Samantha nodded. "I suppose so. Will you be coming back in this coming weekend?"

"Yes, I will."

Suddenly the weekend seemed a long way away, and Samantha was surprised at the sudden twist in her heart at the realization that she wouldn't see Ben Thompson for several days. "Have a good week."

"Thank you. I hope you have a good one, too. And that the work isn't too hard."

She chuckled. "I hope it isn't either. But I guess I'd better get in there and see."

Ben smiled and nodded. "See you Friday."

"See you Friday." Samantha hurried inside, trying to hide how much she hated to see him go.

"You did come," Mrs. Miller greeted her as she took a loaded tray to a nearby table. "I was a little afraid that you'd changed your mind."

She very nearly had the night before when she couldn't keep things from sliding across Faith's tray. But Samantha had given her word, and she never liked to break it. "I've got to try. By the end of the day, you may decide I'm not waitress material."

"Oh, no. There is nothing in this job you can't do, and so what if you drop a loaded tray or break a dish or two? It won't be anything the rest of us haven't done before. It happens in this business."

For a moment, Samantha wondered if the older woman had read her mind, but she knew that was impossible. Evidently accidents were something that happened often enough that they didn't bother Mrs. Miller too much, and Samantha felt relieved that she wouldn't be fired if she dumped a whole tray. But she prayed that wouldn't happen.

The day flew by as she learned what Mrs. Miller expected of her. To begin, the proprietor went to a table with Samantha and showed her how to ask for the order, write it down the way the kitchen liked it, and then turn in the order. But first off, Mrs. Miller looked each of the men at the table in the eye and said, "This is my new waitress, Miss Samantha Carter. You are to treat her with respect and watch your language around her. Is this clear?"

Each man looked from Mrs. Miller to Samantha and back again. They all nodded profusely but seemed to be tongue-tied for the moment.

"Furthermore, she has my permission to dump your food in your lap or on your heads if you get out of line in any way. Is that clear?"

"Yes, ma'am." A man about the same age as Ben and Gabe said, although he did wink at Samantha.

Mrs. Miller raised an eyebrow at him. "None of that either, Nolan Powell."

"It is perfectly clear, Mrs. Miller," the other man of the same age said.

"We won't be gettin' out of line to Miss Samantha," a man who might have been their father said.

"Thank you, I appreciate that."

"And I'll be watching you all to make sure you mind your manners," Mrs. Miller said.

She did the same thing at each and every table Samantha waited on that day, and each and every man who came in promised to treat Samantha with respect. But that didn't stop them from asking if she had a beau and if they could court her. By the end of the day, she'd had ten requests to see her safely home, but she'd refused each one. Obviously the town had a drastic shortage of marriageable women.

Mrs. Miller also helped her bring food to each table and showed her how to put each plate down in front of the customer. After half-a-dozen times, Samantha began to think she really would be able to handle the job.

But she'd had never been so glad to see quitting time come as she was that day. By then, each new step she took shot pain from her foot to her hip, and she was sure her arms might fall off at any moment from carrying the heavy trays. Ben had been right. This job was hard. But she wasn't about to quit. Not now. She had no other prospects for work, and Mrs. Miller did need her. Surely she'd get used to carrying the trays and all the walking in a few days.

When she told Samantha she could go on home, Mrs. Miller added, "We never discussed your schedule and which days you wanted off, but I'm assuming that since Ben Thompson comes into town on the weekends, you might not want to work then?"

"I could probably work awhile on Saturdays, but I would like Sunday off if that is possible," Samantha said. She wasn't sure what to say about Mrs. Miller's remark about Ben. And although she would like Sundays off, Samantha quickly realized her employer was right. She would like to see Ben when he was in town.

"How about this schedule through the week, work on

Saturday until after lunch and all day Sunday off?"

"That will be fine." More than fine. She wasn't expecting to have that much time off, but she certainly welcomed it.

"And I'll have you out of here before supper each night. Sometimes we have some rowdy cowboys in here in the evenings, and I've found it's easier to have men or older women work that shift."

That suited Samantha fine. She had no desire to work at night. That was when she would be able to spend time with Faith and her family and the boarders. "Thank you, I appreciate that."

Mrs. Miller nodded. "You're welcome. I'm glad you're willing to work here at least for a while. We'll be having a busy week with more people coming in for the celebrations this weekend. You go on home and get some rest."

"Thank you, Mrs. Miller. I don't think I'll have a problem sleeping tonight, that's for sure. See you in the morning."

"See you then." Mrs. Miller hurried off in the direction of the kitchen, and Samantha waved good-bye to the other workers. She took a deep breath as she walked outside. How wonderful to have light left in the day.

"How did your first day go, Miss Samantha?" a familiar voice asked.

She turned to find Matt Thompson leaning against the restaurant wall. "Why, Matt, how nice to see you. My day went fine. I'm a bit tired, I must admit, but I didn't drop a thing."

"I was sure you'd do fine. May I walk home with you?"

"Of course. But where is Hope?"

"Oh, she walks home from school with her friends most days. This was on my way home, so I thought I'd see if you might like company if you were about to get off work. And you happened out right as I got here."

"Well, I'm glad of the company." Samantha wondered if his papa had asked him to see her home, but she didn't want to ask. It might put him in an awkward position.

"Did your papa get off this morning?"

"Yes, ma'am. He dropped me and Hope off at school on his way out of town. He said you knew your way to the restaurant real well."

Maybe Ben hadn't told his son to see her home, after all. Still it was nice to have someone to talk to as they walked.

"I think Papa gets a little lonely out on the farm, but he loves what he does. Still, I think he would have liked to have stayed in town a little longer this time."

"I'm sure you all miss each other when you are separated," Samantha said.

"We do. I wish Mrs. Rose's place were a little closer in so we could live with Papa and go to school here. It's not all that far on a weekend, but to go back and forth each day would take a chunk out of Papa's time. And Aunt Faith is glad to have us. It's hard to think of him out there by himself, though. I wish Papa. . ."

Samantha waited for Matt to finish the sentence, but he didn't. And she hadn't known him long enough to prod. But she couldn't help but wonder what it was he was wishing his papa would do.

seven

Ben was disappointed that they hadn't had any news from the marshal about Samantha by the time he left town. He could only keep praying that nothing in her past had her running from the law and that by the time he got back in town, they'd know for sure. Even though he'd known her less than a week, he couldn't deny that he was beginning to feel something for Samantha Carter.

For the first time since he'd begun farming Rose's place, Ben seriously thought maybe he'd made the wrong decision and that he should have stayed in town and worked with Gabe. He couldn't recall when four days had passed so slowly. And it wasn't because he hadn't been busy—he'd found things to do to keep himself working harder than usual. He'd mended tack, helped Homer gather in some of his crops along with his own, and tended his fields better than ever so that his neighbor wouldn't feel as if he were leaving all the work to him.

Even so, those few days passed like a turtle crossing the road because he hadn't been able to turn his mind off what might be going on in town. He missed his children as always and prayed that Matt was doing all right in the apartment by himself, although he was certain his son was doing just fine. Gabe and Faith would have let him know if he wasn't.

Always Ben asked the Lord to watch over his family in his absence. And now he also asked Him to watch over

Samantha. But no matter what he did, visions of that woman filled his mind all week.

On Monday evening Ben had watched the sun go down and wondered what time Samantha got off work and how her first day had gone—and if any of the men had given her a hard time.

On Tuesday morning he'd wondered if she'd seen the sunrise that morning and if she'd made it to work all right—although he was confident she knew the way. That evening he'd wondered how her day had gone and prayed she wasn't working too hard and that no one had caught her eye and that she'd been telling the truth when she'd told the lawyer's wife that she wasn't looking for any man.

On Wednesday morning the sunrise was magnificent, spreading its light across the land, and he'd wished Samantha had seen it with him. He'd hoped she'd have a good day. By that evening he'd wanted nothing more than to get on his horse and go check on her. . .his children. . .everything in town.

By noon on Thursday, it was all he could do to keep from packing his things and going in early. The only thing that stopped him was seeing Homer head up the road toward the house, bringing a cast-iron pot with him.

"Wondered if you might want to share some of this stew I made. With the wife and children still gone, I can't eat it all."

"Why I'd be glad to, Homer. I was wondering what I was going to make myself. Come on in."

Ben grabbed bowls and spoons, and Homer dipped out the hearty beef and potato stew. They bowed their heads, and Ben said the blessing. "Lord, we thank You for this day, for the food You've provided. We ask You to watch over our families and help us to do Your will. It's in Jesus' name we pray. Amen."

"Amen," Homer echoed.

Ben took a bite of the stew. "This is good, Homer. Thanks for thinking of me."

"Well, I figured you were as lonesome as I am. I never thought about it much until the wife went to see her family, but it must be real hard on you to be by yourself out here all the time."

"It wasn't at first," Ben admitted, "but lately it's been getting harder every day."

"After these last few weeks, I can sure see how it would be. Have you given any consideration to finding a wife?"

"Not until recently. There aren't many single women of the marrying kind out this way. But. . ."

"But?"

"Well, something happened on the way into town last week."

"What was that?"

While they ate, Ben filled Homer in on the story of Samantha. Homer let him tell it all and then sat back in his chair and grinned. "You mean you took her to be a boy?"

"Well, she was dressed like one. But she sure didn't look like a boy once she cleaned up and put on one of Faith's dresses."

"And she's staying at your sister's boardinghouse now? And working at one of the restaurants?"

"Yes."

"You don't sound very happy about that."

"Oh I'm glad she's staying at Faith's. It's the working at the restaurant that I'm not too pleased about."

"Hmm. I see." Homer ladled more stew into each of their bowls. "Afraid of the competition in town, are you?"

Suddenly Ben knew that was exactly what had been worrying him—that some man would catch her eye and begin to court her before he could get back into town. "Well yes, I think I am. But she's said she isn't looking for a man."

"That doesn't mean she won't find one."

"Thanks, Homer." Ben's heart dove to the bottom of his stomach.

"Why, you can be that man, Ben. You saved her life. If she's going to be lookin' at anyone that way, I'd think it would be you."

"You think I might have a chance?"

"Ben, you're a good man. Why wouldn't she consider you?"

"I don't know. Matt thinks I should try to court her."

"Well, if you don't want some other man to beat you to it, you might consider asking her."

"It's been a long time—and well, I don't think I actually asked to court my Molly. We sort of ended up together."

"You did ask her to marry you, didn't you?"

"Well of course, but by then, we just kind of knew we'd marry. We were raised next door to each other."

"Oh, well that is different. And now you are interested in a complete stranger."

"Yes. I am interested in Samantha Carter." There. He'd said it out loud.

"Well, you'd better at least start hinting that you might want to court her, don't you think? At least so that she'll know you're interested. Women don't like to wonder about those things, you know."

"I guess maybe I should. I'm going into town first thing

tomorrow morning. Want to come with me? You can stay at the apartment with Matt and me."

"I'm sure tempted to do that. But I'd better get the house cleaned up. Wife will be back next week, and I've kind of let the place go. Besides, there are all those celebrations tomorrow, and I don't like the crowds. But I sure will be waiting to hear how it goes. You can be certain of that. And don't worry about the place if you decide to stay an extra day or so. I'll look after it. You ought to go on in this afternoon so you'll be there for all those festivities tomorrow."

"You know, I think I might do that. Thanks, Homer." Ben decided right then and there that he couldn't wait until the next day. He was going to Guthrie that very afternoon. And he sure hoped to have good news to report back to Homer when he came back.

&

The week was one of the most tiring of Samantha's life. She missed teaching—at least then she could get off her feet from time to time and sit at her desk. The restaurant was constantly busy with more and more people coming in to celebrate Guthrie becoming the official capital of the Oklahoma Territory. When one table was cleared, it was immediately taken by the next in line. It was hard to tell when the breakfast bunch turned into the lunch bunch except by what they began to order.

Samantha was so busy the hours flew, but she was so exhausted by the end of those first few days she was sure she fell asleep before her head ever hit the pillow at night. By Thursday her feet didn't bother her quite so bad, but her arms were still sore from lifting the heavy trays.

Tired as she was, Samantha found herself thinking about

Ben Thompson more than once during that first week at work and as she got to know his children better. Hope was a joy to be around, and so was Matt.

On Thursday as they walked home, he said, "I can't wait for Papa to get back in town tomorrow. I hope he doesn't miss the parade and everything. I heard that Governor Steele came in at 4:00 a.m. and that he's been at the Noble Hotel since then."

"That's what I heard, too. I'm excited to see the parade and all tomorrow. Mrs. Miller is closing the restaurant for the festivities."

"That's good. It'd sure be a shame to miss seeing it all."

"Yes, it would. Does your papa know what time the parade will start?"

"I'm sure he does. He keeps up with the news pretty well, and it's been in the papers for weeks now."

Samantha hoped Ben did. She'd hate to see him miss it—his family was looking forward to joining the crowds. She and Matt continued talking about all kinds of things on the way home.

Home. That's what Faith's boardinghouse had become to Samantha. She loved living there. It was the closest she'd come to having a real home in years. Her parents had both died in a train accident when she was off at school. Just after that her brother had married, and his wife had hounded him to move back to Ohio, where she was from. Samantha wasn't asked to go with them, and she'd stayed with her grandmother while she finished school. Her grandmother had passed away right after graduation, and Samantha had been on her own ever since.

She'd been glad to get a teaching job in Kansas when she

got out of school, and the boardinghouse she'd lived in had been nice, but it hadn't had the homey feel of Faith's place. Now she looked forward to coming home each night and answering questions about her day as Faith made supper. She tried to help with the supper preparations as much as they'd let her, which wasn't much, but it made her feel like part of the family. Today, however, Faith had most of her preparations underway and told Samantha to sit and relax. She loved sitting in the kitchen and listening to the family talk. But today, Hope was having trouble with a math problem.

"I've always been pretty good at math. Would you like me to help?" Samantha asked.

"Oh yes, if you don't mind." The relieved look on Hope's face said how frustrated she was.

"Not at all." Samantha pulled the book and Hope's tablet to her. "Oh, you didn't carry over all the way. Look." She quickly showed Hope where she'd missed a figure. "That's all it was."

Hope chuckled. "I guess I got in too big a hurry. Math doesn't come easy to me for some reason. Uncle Gabe is good to help and Papa of course when he's in town, but I don't always like to bother them." Her voice lowered a notch. "And I don't really want Matt to know I'm so bad at it."

"I understand. But you can come to me anytime, Hope. I'll be glad to help."

"Thank you, Miss Samantha."

"You're welcome."

Hope took her book and tablet and put them away before going to set the dining room table. Once she was out of the room, Faith turned to Samantha. "See. You don't always have to be helping with kitchen stuff. It was nice of you to help Hope. Sometimes they need help right when I'm in the middle of cooking or of something I can't let go of right away, and I feel bad. And sometimes, I simply don't have the answers. Now I'll send them to you."

"I hope you do." And Samantha did. She missed teaching very much—more than she ever had believed she would. "If you are sure I can't help with anything else, I'll go freshen up."

"You go on. Supper isn't for half an hour yet."

Samantha hurried upstairs as fast as she could, considering how tired she was. If Ben was here, he'd be able to see how right he'd been about how hard the waitressing job was. Her back hurt by the end of the day, and the muscles in her neck and shoulders sometimes seemed tied in knots. Even so, she didn't want to admit it to anyone but herself. If Annie had been here, she would have told her—she missed her friend a lot. But she certainly didn't want to complain to Ben's family.

Hard as the work was, though, she did like the Millers and the others she worked with. So far no one had made any untoward advances to her, but she'd received offers to see her home each day and was glad she could truthfully tell them she had someone else seeing her safely home.

She freshened up and repinned her hair before going back downstairs. She headed toward the kitchen, but the sound of a familiar voice caused her heart to jump and then pound ever so hard. Ben had come in early! She couldn't keep from smiling and told herself it was because his children would be so happy to see him, but none of that excused the way her pulse began racing the closer she got to the kitchen.

He was surrounded by Matt and Hope and his sister, each

pelting him with all kinds of questions, but he looked up the moment she walked in the kitchen, caught her glance, and held it. Something in the way he looked at her turned her heart to pure mush, and Samantha knew she was as glad as his children were that he was back.

☙

When Ben's gaze met Samantha's from across the kitchen, he knew exactly why he'd come into Guthrie early. He wanted to see how she was, if the job was too much for her, if any of the men had given her any trouble—if any of the men had caught her eye.

Her smile told him she was doing well, and he was glad of that. He wasn't sure how he was going to find out all the rest he wanted to know without asking, but maybe he'd be able to see for himself over the next few days.

"Matt was hoping that you would get here in time for the festivities tomorrow. I'm glad to see that you have," Samantha said.

"It's not every day that one's city becomes the capital of a territory. We were all here at the beginning. I didn't want to miss out on all the fun. I figured I might as well join my family for the celebrations."

"I'm glad you did," Faith said. "It's going to be a great day. And it is special. We helped to settle this town, and we'll help keep it going through your children and ours."

It took a minute for his sister's words to sink it. "Faith?" He looked from her to Gabe. The grin on his brother-in-law's face pretty much told him what he wanted to know. His suspicions were confirmed by the delicate blush creeping up his sister's face along with the tears of happiness that shone in her eyes. "I'm going to be an uncle?"

Faith half laughed, half sobbed, as she nodded. "You are. At last."

Ben's throat filled with the need to laugh or cry himself as he bent down and gave his sister a hug. "I know you've waited a long time for this and thought it would never happen. I can't begin to tell you how happy I am for you, sis."

Hope and Matt wanted their turn to congratulate their aunt, as did Rose and Samantha, even though she probably didn't know that Faith had believed she'd never be able to have a child and that Gabe had accepted that fact when he asked her to marry him. Ben gave Faith one more hug and then turned to give his brother-in-law a good-natured slap on the back.

"Congratulations, Gabe. The Lord has blessed your marriage in a big way. I hope I'm as good an uncle to your child as you've been to my children."

"Oh, we don't have any doubts about that. We've been holding this news in for a while, but Faith felt this weekend was the perfect time to tell everyone."

"I'm glad I came in early, if only to hear it."

"She wouldn't have brought it up if you hadn't been here, Ben. You were the one who asked her to come to Guthrie with you, Matt, and Hope. And you were the one who told me that she thought she couldn't have children and not to let her know how I felt about her unless I could accept that we might never have a child. If not for you, we would never have found each other. There's no way we could have announced this news if you weren't here to hear it."

"Oh my," Faith said, wiping her eyes. "I guess I should have waited to tell our good news until after supper. I just couldn't wait any longer. But if I don't get food on the table soon, our boarders are not going to be very happy."

"We'll help," Samantha said, "and everyone will understand. Thank you for letting me in on your good news."

"You feel like family, Samantha," Faith said.

"And you are as much family as I am, even though we're both boarders," Rose added.

Ben could tell by Samantha's smile that she was pleased to be considered family, and he didn't much mind that she felt that way.

eight

As Ben and his family, along with Rose and Samantha, watched the beginning of the day's celebrations, he couldn't help but feel a sense of pride that his family had helped to settle Guthrie. He was especially happy that Samantha was able to share the day with them.

The governor's procession started downtown on Oklahoma Avenue at two o'clock sharp and headed east toward Capitol Square. Ben looked over Samantha's head to see that behind Governor Steele, a parade of carriages, special delegations, military troops, bands, and people either riding horses or walking fell in behind him.

School was out for the day, and many families had come in early to picnic near Cottonwood Creek. Now thousands of people lined the street on both sides, three, four, and in some places five deep to watch the parade. Once it passed them, they fell in line to follow it to the square where they would hear the governor's speech.

By the time Ben and his party got to the square, some of the less notable speakers had finished, which was no great disappointment to any of them. The new governor began his speech by saying how flattered he was when the president asked him to accept the governorship of the territory and how he wanted to be the best governor he could be. He said he would do all he could for the people living there and that he would do his duty as honestly as he could.

Each pause he took was filled with much applause and cheering, and in conclusion, he thanked everyone for welcoming him. Then he and his entourage were rushed off to a lavish reception that had been planned in his honor. Later that evening, he would attend the first inaugural ball of the territory.

Ben, along with his family and friends, returned to the boardinghouse to finish celebrating that Guthrie was the official capital in their own way. When they walked into the kitchen, the mouthwatering aroma of the roast Faith had put on earlier that day greeted them, and Faith, Hope, Rose, and Samantha all pitched in to help finish up the meal.

The table was set and Faith was ready to serve by the time the rest of the boarders returned. They'd watched the parade in another area of town to make sure they were some of the first in line for the reception. Everyone was happy to talk about what they'd seen and heard.

"I wish you'd stayed for the reception," Mrs. Fairmont said. "It was so nice, and I've never seen so many dignitaries in one place in my life. Why didn't you all go?"

"Faith was getting a bit tired," Gabe said.

Ben couldn't miss the protective look Gabe gave his wife. He'd felt the same way with Molly. . .especially in those first days after he'd found out they'd be having a child.

"It was a long day," Mrs. Warner said. "I couldn't believe how many people from all the outlying areas were lined up to meet the governor."

"Well, we townspeople weren't the only ones who made the run and claimed land that day," Gabe said. "Many went as far out as they could go and still be able to come in for supplies."

"Yes. My man was determined to have a farm," Rose said.

"And a finer piece of land couldn't be found, Rose," Ben said. "It takes all kinds to settle a new land—townspeople, farmers, and ranchers, too. It took us all to settle this territory. Now that it's official, we'll be a state one of these days. Won't that be something to celebrate?"

"It will for certain." Faith smiled. "I'm so thankful that our child will be born here."

Gabe reached over and took Faith's hand and brought it to his lips. "So am I."

"You are—?" Mrs. Fairmont started.

"There's going to be a baby?" Mrs. Warner finished.

They hadn't been in on the announcement the night before. Faith had wanted to savor the moment before telling them, but now her smile told them all.

"Yes. Around the New Year, Doc says."

"Oh dear, how exciting!" Mrs. Warner looked at Mrs. Fairmont. "We'll have to start knitting soon."

"Yes, we will. We'll go shopping next week."

Ben stole a glance at Samantha and found her smiling at his sister and brother-in-law. How could one not? They were in love and expecting their first child. He saw his own children smiling at them and was glad that Hope and Matt could see how happy Faith and Gabe were together. They needed good examples of married life to draw from and learn what it was they wanted in a marriage one day. Their mother had passed away when they were too young to realize what a wonderful marriage he and Molly had, but at least for now, they had that example while living in town with their aunt and uncle.

Ben looked back at Samantha and saw her gaze was on him. Her face flushed as she turned away, as if she was embarrassed to be caught staring at him when he'd been doing the same thing to her most of the day. He might pay the marshal a visit tomorrow and see what he'd found out about Samantha. He had to know if anything in her past would force him to tamp down his growing attraction to her. And he wanted to know now.

❧

Samantha wished she didn't have to work the next day, but at least it was only a half day. Ben offered to accompany her to work because he had errands in town that he needed to do. She was quite glad to share his company, in spite of the fact that she still felt she must guard her heart.

After witnessing Gabe and Faith's happiness these last few days, she had to admit she longed for a love of her own. But she still wasn't sure she could trust any man with her heart. How did one know for certain?

"Faith told me you helped Hope with her math the other day," Ben said, his voice interrupting her thoughts. "Thank you. That's one of the things I hate about being apart from them when school is in session—not being able to help them like that."

"You are welcome. I was glad to do it. Math has always come easy to me for some reason. Mrs. Miller has already complimented me on always having my tickets added up right."

"How is the work? With all that's gone on this weekend, I haven't had a chance to ask."

And Samantha had been hoping he wouldn't. "It's going well. You were right. It is a little harder than I anticipated, but I'm getting used to it. And the Millers are wonderful to work for. They don't allow any foul language or rowdiness in the restaurant."

"That's a good thing. I imagine a lot of that kind of thing goes on in some places."

"That's what Mrs. Miller said. But she won't abide it. Why, only the other day she had her husband throw a man out of the place." She didn't tell Ben that the man was giving her a hard time, insisting that he was the man for her and promising her all manner of things if she'd just come away with him right then.

"I'm glad to hear it. How many proposals have you had?"

Samantha couldn't help but chuckle. "I've lost count. But certainly none I'd ever consider."

"You wouldn't accept a proposal without courting someone first, would you?"

"Why no. But I'm not ready for that yet. I—"

"You don't have to explain to me, Sam." Ben let the name slip from his tongue without realizing it. "I didn't mean to make you feel uncomfortable."

"It's all right. I. . .haven't seen many examples of a happy marriage since my parents passed away, except for Faith and Gabe. I keep thinking about that poor lawyer's wife and how she couldn't trust her own husband. And I've met men, even at the restaurant, who I know are married, but they don't seem to care if they honor their vows. I don't want to rush into marriage with anyone. I want to get to know someone well enough to feel I can trust him, and I want to know without a doubt that we love each other like Faith and Gabe do."

Ben nodded. "I think you are right about that. Faith and Gabe cared about each other long before they came to trust their love. Molly and I knew each other a long time. . .all our lives, really. I don't think one has to know someone that long to be sure, but it doesn't hurt to take your time to get to know each other."

"Thank you, Ben. It's always nice to have confirmation of one's opinions." That was the first time he'd mentioned his wife to her, and she was gratified that he felt comfortable talking to her about his personal life. Yet she couldn't help wondering if he'd ever be ready to marry again or if his love for his wife would keep him from doing so. Her heart gave a little twist, and she wasn't sure if it was from sympathy for him or for herself.

By then they'd arrived at the restaurant, and Ben looked down at her. "I'm going to be in town for a while. I'll come back and see you home, since Matt isn't in school today."

"Oh, then you did tell him to see me home. I was wondering about that."

"Matt likes seeing you home," Ben said, avoiding her question completely. "And I'm looking forward to it, too. What time do you get off?"

"I believe Mrs. Miller said around one or two. Probably depends on how busy we are." She peeked in the window. "And from the looks of it, we're going to be busy."

"I'll be back to check in." Ben tipped his hat and turned away. "Don't work too hard."

"I'll try not to." Samantha hurried inside and donned her apron, but with a short day and a handsome escort home to look forward to, she went to work with a smile on her face and a thankful heart for this man who showed such concern for her.

ᕗ

Ben went straight to the marshal's office after he dropped Samantha off at the restaurant. With all the goings on in town, it didn't surprise him to find the man out of the office, but it did frustrate him no little bit. Determined to catch up with the marshal before he went back to the farm, Ben headed to Gabe's office to talk about it. When he opened the door, he found the marshal sitting by Gabe's desk.

"I just missed you, Marshal," Ben said as he pulled another chair up to Gabe's desk. "I take it you have news for us?"

"Well, better yet, I have no news for you. There is nothing on Miss Samantha Carter. And there's nothing on a young Sam Carter as she called herself dressed as a young man. If she's guilty of any crime, it would have to be under a different name."

Ben's heart dove into his stomach. He hadn't thought of that.

"But I don't think that's the case. I don't think she would have introduced herself with a shorter name for Samantha if it were. I think you can both assume that, while she might have wanted to get away from something or someone, she isn't guilty of any crime."

Ben really hadn't believed Sam could be guilty of anything bad. Still, the marshal's words were the ones he wanted to hear, and the relief he felt was huge.

"I can see that matters even more to you than it does me, Ben," Gabe said.

"Probably."

"Is this Miss Carter the one who works at Miller's Restaurant?" the marshal asked.

"It is."

"Well, I can see why it could matter to a man who might be thinking of taking a wife."

"It could." Ben knew he wasn't hiding a thing from these

two men. But he wasn't going to admit to anyone but himself that he was eager to get back to the restaurant and see for himself how things were going for Sam. "Mostly it's good to know that we have nothing to worry about given that she's living at my sister's with my daughter under the same roof."

"He's right, Marshal. Not that we thought Samantha had a criminal past, but when it comes to our loved ones, we needed to be sure."

"Well, I'm glad I could tell you she's in the clear." The marshal stood up and stretched. "Guess I'd better get back to the office. Last night was a late one, with all the hoopla over the governor. Thankfully, everything went off relatively peaceable, especially with so many strangers in town."

"How long before you think things will return to normal around here?" Gabe asked.

"Probably next week. Most people will need to get back home and get on with their lives. But I'm glad I was here to witness Guthrie finally being the official capital of Oklahoma Territory. Gentlemen, we can say we were here at the beginning. Not many can claim to have settled a town overnight."

"How true that is," Ben said. "I'll walk out with you, Marshal. I have a few things to attend to today. See you later, Gabe."

His brother-in-law was standing, too. "All right. I've got to check on the Beadle place and look at the lay of the land over at the Stewart place. We're going to level ground on it starting Monday."

They headed off in different directions, and Ben was kind of glad. He intended to have his lunch at Miller's Restaurant, and he didn't want company. He did stop at

Kimball Grocery and put in an order for some canned goods to pick up on Monday morning; then he went to Randall & Lyon Hardware to order more nails. After that, he couldn't think of anything else he needed to do before he went to the restaurant.

It was high noon, and Miller's Restaurant was even more crowded than usual, but Mrs. Miller found him a table in Sam's section. "I can't tell you how happy I am to have Samantha working here, Ben. Thank you for bringing her in."

"I didn't bring her so you would hire her. I only wanted to feed her."

"Ben Thompson, I know you aren't happy about her working here, but if she was going to end up waiting tables anyway, at least be glad it's here. You know we're going to watch over her as well as you would."

"I'm sorry. You're right, Mrs. Miller. I am glad for that."

"Well good. And I've not said a word, but you aren't fooling me for a minute, young man. You have your eye on Samantha every bit as much as these other men do. Only difference is, you might have a chance one day. These others are just plain out of luck."

"You couldn't have told me anything I'd rather hear," Ben said with a grin.

"Does she know how you—"

"No one knows how I feel. And I don't think she's ready for me to let her know. You'll be sure and let me know if some man comes in and gets her attention while I'm at the farm, right? I might need to speed things up if that was to happen."

Mrs. Miller handed him a menu. "I'll let you know. Samantha will be right over to take your order."

"Thanks, Mrs. Miller."

"You're welcome." She turned and went to seat the next people in line.

"Why hello, Ben. What can I get for you today?"

Samantha was looking down at him with a smile that he hoped she didn't greet all her customers with. It was heart-stopping sweet, and he didn't much like the idea that other men might be the recipients of it. "What do you recommend?"

"Well, the stew looks real good, and everyone says it is. But the fried chicken is a favorite, too."

"Hmm. Wonder what Faith is planning for supper?"

"I don't know." Samantha laughed. "Why don't you go with something light? You know Faith is going to have one of your favorites. She told me that she always tries to make those for you when you come into town."

"And what is my favorite? Did she tell you that?"

"I believe it was that roast beef you had last night. And after that, it is her fried chicken."

"You must listen well or be very observant."

"I try to do both."

Ben knew he was keeping her too long at his table, and he didn't want Mrs. Miller storming over and accusing him of doing exactly that, embarrassing Sam and himself, so he quickly decided on the stew.

"I'll get it right out for you."

Ben watched her leave, but he didn't miss that half-a-dozen other men did the same thing. Still, he remembered what Mrs. Miller had told him. None of them had caught her eye—at least not yet. And Matt would still be seeing her home. He could breathe easy for now.

It wasn't long before Sam brought his meal, and he ate as slowly as he could, watching customers come and go until Sam came back to see if he wanted dessert. He didn't need it; that was for sure. But he wasn't ready to leave, so he ordered a big slice of Mrs. Miller's famous apple pie. He hoped Sam got off work soon because once he finished that pie, he didn't think he'd be able to eat anything more.

He was very relieved when Sam brought his pie and a bowl of stew. For a minute, he thought she was going to drop off his pie quickly and deliver the stew to another table. But she set the stew down across from him and handed the tray to a passing waiter.

"Would you mind some company? Mrs. Miller said I'm officially off work."

"I'd be honored." Ben quickly stood up and pulled out a chair for her. "I'll even share my pie with you if you'd like."

"Why, that is nice of you. You got the last piece of apple until Mrs. Miller makes some more." She took her seat and let him push it in. "So I might want a little bite."

Ben took his sweet time eating that pie as Sam ate her lunch. He wasn't in any hurry to go anywhere. And if some of those love-struck cowboys thought he was courting Miss Samantha Carter, that was fine by him.

nine

The next few weeks flew by for Samantha. Most of the regulars at the restaurant had quit asking to either see her home or come courting, and for that she was very grateful. But every now and again, someone new would come in for a few days, and it would all start up again.

Mrs. Miller had told her they all thought Ben Thompson was courting her.

"He isn't. Not that I know of anyway. I think he feels responsible for saving my life."

"What would you think if he did ask to court you?"

Samantha shook her head. "I'm not sure. I haven't been looking for a husband, and to be truthful, what I've seen of marriage besides with my own parents, Faith and Gabe, and you and Mr. Miller hasn't been great. I want what all of you have, and well, I'm not sure that Ben isn't still pining for his Molly."

"Oh, a part of him will probably always love her. But that doesn't mean he can't love another woman, Samantha. And I sense that Ben longs for a wife again."

"Really?"

"Yes, really."

"But. . .I. . ."

"You're still unsure about things. That's understandable. But there are many good marriages out there, Samantha. I'd like to think there are more good ones than bad."

"I suppose I'm not sure how good a wife I'd make. And from all accounts, Molly was a wonderful wife and mother. I'm not sure I could live up to her memory."

"I'm sure you'd make a fine wife. Ben doesn't seem the type to compare."

"But how do I know? How can I be sure?"

"I think you take it to the Lord, Samantha. Ask Him to guide you and help you to know."

Samantha realized that was the best advice she could receive and that she should have been praying about it long before now. "Thank you, Mrs. Miller. I appreciate being able to talk to you about this. Faith is wonderful, but she's Ben's sister and—"

"No need to explain, Samantha. You come to me any time. And for what it's worth, I think Ben Thompson is sweet on you, and it doesn't have a thing to do with saving your life."

"You think so?"

"I do. It won't surprise me one bit if one of these days he asks to court you for real. You might think it over so you have an answer when he does."

"Yes, ma'am." Samantha wasn't sure Mrs. Miller was right about Ben wanting to court her, but the very idea sent her pulse to racing as she headed for home with Matt. If she looked a little flushed, she was glad the young man didn't mention it.

As Hope had been doing off and on since the first time she'd asked for help, that afternoon she brought more math problems to Samantha. Hope was bringing home better grades, and Samantha was very happy to have helped with that.

When Hope went upstairs to finish her work before

coming back down to set the table, Faith turned to Samantha. "You know, you'd make a very good teacher. Have you ever considered that?"

"I have. In fact. . ." Samantha didn't want to lie. But she didn't want to go into why she'd left Kansas either.

"You *are* a teacher, aren't you, Samantha?" Faith asked, turning from the stove.

"Yes. I taught in Kansas for several years before I came here. But when I came to Guthrie, the school year was already in session, and well, I didn't figure they'd need a teacher." That was true enough. Hopefully Faith wouldn't ask anything about why she had left.

"Oh, I'm sure they'd be glad to have an experienced teacher, Samantha, especially for next session. I've heard one of the teachers is getting married."

"Really?" Samantha could not deny that she really missed teaching. Her biggest fear was that somehow her former principal had started a campaign to ruin her reputation all the way to Guthrie, even though he had no way of knowing she'd come here.

"Really. I'll do some more checking. It would be so much easier on you."

"Well, that's for sure. I'd still be on my feet some, but nothing like at the restaurant."

"And you'd have complete weekends off, and holidays, too—spring and fall breaks."

"I know." It was one of the things she'd always loved about teaching. "Maybe I'll apply for a position, if you find out they want someone."

"I'll see what I can find out first thing tomorrow."

"Samantha, dear?" Mrs. Warner peeked her head around

the kitchen door. "There's a gentleman here to see you."

"A man to see me?" Samantha couldn't imagine who might be calling. She'd refused all offers to do so since she'd been working for Mrs. Miller. Suddenly her heart seemed to stop beating. Surely Principal Jennings hadn't found her here.

"Yes, he appears to be your age and quite good-looking— through these old eyes of mine, anyway."

Samantha breathed a sigh of relief. It couldn't be her old principal. He was at least fifteen years older than she was. But manners insisted that she see who was at the door, and she hurried down the hall to find out who was calling. She was a little surprised to see Darrell Magee, a young attorney who'd been coming into Miller's Restaurant for the past month. He hadn't actually asked to court her. It appeared he was so confident that he didn't feel he had to ask.

"Good evening, Miss Carter. I hope I haven't come at a bad time."

Samantha didn't consider just before supper to be a good time to call, but she only asked, "What can I do for you, Mr. Magee?"

The man turned his hat around in his hands and gave her a self-assured smile. "Well, I was wondering if you'd like to go for a walk with me. There's an ice-cream parlor downtown, and I—"

"I'm sorry, Mr. Magee, but we are about to sit down to supper, and well, even if we weren't, I'd have to say no. Thank you for your invitation, though."

He looked at her as if he couldn't believe she'd turned him down. "Are you quite sure, Miss Carter?"

"Why yes, I am. I am not used to gentlemen calling on me without getting permission first, Mr. Magee. And at present,

I've given no one that permission."

"That's what I've been told. But I wagered that they were wrong. I guess I lost."

"You wagered on whether I would go walking out with you?"

"Yes, ma'am, I did. Will you reconsider? I'd be very beholden to you."

"No, sir. I will not. Good evening." Samantha showed him to the door and slammed it shut behind him. The gall of the man!

❧

Ben headed toward Guthrie, fully aware that he'd lived from one weekend to the next over the last few months. Sam wasn't letting anyone court her, but from what Mrs. Miller had told him, it didn't stop any of the men who came into the restaurant from giving it their all. And when one man gave up, another quickly came to take his place. He'd come to realize that there always would be another man in line, especially with a beautiful single lady like Samantha.

And while he left Guthrie at the end of each weekend relieved that she hadn't given anyone any encouragement, by the end of the next workweek, he'd convinced himself that the situation might have changed while he was gone. He didn't breathe easy until he'd sat in the café awhile and seen for himself that she didn't seem taken with anyone.

Deep down he knew that if anyone had come calling for her at the boardinghouse, Faith would be sure to let him know. He should be able to relax and know that both Mrs. Miller and Faith would look out for his best interests. . .even if he hadn't come right out and told them about his feelings for Samantha. Mrs. Miller had made it clear he was hiding nothing from her, and he was pretty sure his sister knew how he felt about Sam, too.

Still, Samantha hadn't given him any real sign that she was looking to be courted, and he was beginning to wonder if maybe he should give her more than a hint that he was falling in love with her—so far what he'd thought he was hinting had seemed to have fallen on deaf ears. Or was she ignoring his hints so that she didn't have to come out and say she wasn't interested? He hoped not. He really thought Sam was more forthright than that. More than likely, he wasn't doing it right. But he'd better learn. Maybe it was time to ask his sister how he should go about it.

Before long, he'd be too busy to go into Guthrie on Thursday nights. And once harvest was upon them, he might not be able to make it in on weekends at all. His crops were doing well. They'd had the right amount of rain and sun, and he figured he'd have a bumper crop of cane and sweet corn.

But if he didn't get in until Friday or even Saturday, someone else might catch Sam's eye and have more of a chance to make his case without Ben in the picture. Maybe he'd talk to Faith this weekend.

He spurred Rusty on toward town. His faithful horse could get there with his eyes closed by now—or at least with Ben's eyes closed. He had no doubt that Rusty would deliver him to his sister's back door no matter what the weather or the condition of his rider. But as they rounded the corner, Ben sat up straight at the sight of a man not much younger than him hurrying up the front walk. Was he too late, after all? Had Samantha allowed some new man to come calling?

He slipped off Rusty's back as soon as his horse stopped in the backyard and barely took time to tie him to one of the hitching posts before hurrying inside his sister's kitchen.

When he opened the back door, it was to find his sister and Mrs. Warner at the door leading into the hall. They both jumped when he shut the door, but when his sister saw it was him, she put a finger over her lips, and he froze right where he was.

He was certain they were eavesdropping on the conversation at the front door, and since Samantha wasn't there and his daughter was too young for callers, he could only surmise that the man he'd seen earlier had indeed come calling. Ben wasn't prepared for the surge of jealousy that flooded his being at the very thought that someone had caught Sam's eye. Suddenly Faith hurried back to the stove, and Mrs. Warner quickly sat down at the kitchen table.

But when Sam pushed open the kitchen door and he saw the stormy expression in her eyes, he began to breathe a little easier. If she cared about that suitor, surely she wouldn't look so angry.

"How dare the man!"

Ben was still over by the back door, and he didn't think Sam had seen him yet. He couldn't help but think how pretty she looked all flushed and in a temper. He was very glad her anger wasn't directed at him.

"Who was it, and what did he do?" Faith asked.

"His name is Darrell Magee. He's an attorney and has been coming into the restaurant for the past several weeks. But never once did he ask to come calling. He just showed up—as part of a wager, I might add!"

Faith gasped. "They had a bet on his chances of seeing you?"

"Evidently so."

"I'm sure you turned him down," Mrs. Warner said.

Ben was certain she and his sister must have already heard what was going on. But of course they weren't going to say so.

"I did. He'll not be coming back. At least he'd better not."

All Ben could think of was that she'd turned the man down. *Thank You, Lord.* "Would you like me or Gabe to have a talk with him?"

Sam started. "Ben! I didn't know you were here."

"You were busy putting that gentleman in his place." He couldn't help but grin. At least his fears that someone had caught her eye were laid to rest. . .for now, anyway. "I'll be glad to tell him not to bother you again."

"Thank you, Ben. But I'm hoping I took care of it."

He hoped she had, too. Because if not, he'd make it quite clear to Mr. Magee that he wasn't to bother her again. "Well, if you change your mind. . ."

Gabe and Matt chose that moment to come into the kitchen from outside.

"Who was that man we just saw leave?" Gabe asked. "Is something wrong?"

"Nothing's wrong, Gabe." At this moment everything was right. But Ben had made up his mind. He was going to talk to his sister as soon as he could get her alone. He wanted to find out if she thought he had any chance at all with Sam. And if she believed he did, he needed to find out how to make sure she was right. Because he didn't want to take a chance on losing her to the next man who decided to come calling on his own.

❧

"It was only an unwanted suitor calling on Samantha. But she took care of it," Faith said, as she pulled roast chicken out of the oven.

"I'm surprised we haven't had more of them show up," Gabe said. "I've been prepared to run them off. Guess I didn't get home in time. I'm sorry, Samantha."

"Until tonight, I've let any of those asking to walk me home or come calling know I wasn't interested. This man fell prey to a wager, which made it worse than if he'd come calling on his own."

"I'm glad you sent him packing," Ben said. "The kind of man who makes a wager on whether a woman will let him court her or not isn't all that noble in my opinion. You be sure and let one of us know if he keeps bothering you, all right?"

Seeing Ben standing there, such a contrast to the man she'd turned away, made Samantha realize that he was the one she'd been measuring all other men by ever since she'd come to Guthrie. And none of them came close. "I will," she promised.

Her face flushed, remembering the conversation with Mrs. Miller. Something in the way Ben was looking at her made her wonder if it was possible her employer was right about Ben being sweet on her. Could Ben think of her as more than the woman who'd tried to pass herself off as a young man, the one he'd saved from a fire? First impressions were hard to get around.

For Samantha, he would always be special because he saved her life. Her heart never failed to give a little twist when she thought back on that day.

But over time Ben had become special to her for many other reasons: caring enough about her to have his son see her home, voicing concern over how difficult she found her work, offering to come to her aid about anything—even talking to an unwanted suitor. Ben Thompson had wound his way into her heart, and she was pretty sure no other man could take his place.

Yet based on what Faith had told her once, Ben was ten years older than she. From time to time, she'd wondered if he thought of her as a child he had to protect. She never wanted him to think of her in that way. But if he thought of her the way Mrs. Miller said he did, wouldn't he have let her know. . . asked to court her?

Then again, he saw her each time he was in town, so there'd be no need to ask to come calling. He could talk to her whenever he wanted. How had he gone about courting Molly? He'd said they'd known each other a long time. Maybe he didn't remember how to actually go about courting after all that time and having had only one woman in his life. Samantha's heart leaped with hope. Maybe he did care but wasn't quite sure how to go about letting a woman know he was interested. And how could she go about finding out without coming right out and asking?

ten

Samantha was glad to have Ben's company on the way home from work on Friday. He'd come in for pie and coffee midafternoon and visited with several townspeople he knew before going off to do a few errands and then coming back to pick her up.

She was pleased that Darrell saw her leave the restaurant with Ben. Maybe he'd think she and Ben were courting and realize that his attentions truly were unwelcome.

Ben pulled her hand through his arm and looked down at her. "I saw that Magee person. Did he give you any trouble today?"

"No. Actually, he apologized to me for what happened. I accepted his apology, but when he asked once more if he could come calling, I told him no, in no uncertain terms."

"I'm glad to hear it."

His words gave her courage to say, "I've been told that some of the men think you are courting me."

"Do they?" He smiled and raised an eyebrow.

"That's what I've heard." There, she'd said it. She held her breath, waiting to see Ben's reaction.

"Does it bother you that they do?" His steps slowed.

"Not at all, I—" Samantha clamped down on her tongue. Here she was about to let him know how she felt about him when her whole purpose for bringing up the subject was to find out how *he* felt about her.

"I'm glad it doesn't bother you. I know you said you weren't looking for a man, and I fully believe you. But, Sam?"

"Yes?" Had she said all that? Oh, yes. . .that day at the law office. Was that why—

"If you ever decide you might be ready to have someone court you, do you think you could consider letting it be me?"

Her heart seemed to expand to near bursting. "I believe I could."

Ben pulled her hand a little farther through his arm. "Will you let me know when that time comes?"

"Yes Ben, I will." She wanted to tell him that now was the time, but she didn't want to say so until she was absolutely sure she could be the kind of wife Ben needed—and that she could accept that she might never measure up to his Molly.

For now, she let herself bask in knowing that he wanted to court her. *Thank You, Lord. Please help me to know if this is Your will for us.*

After that, they talked about the upcoming Independence Day celebrations. The Fourth was on a Friday this year, and that made it easier for Ben to come into town for the day. They were all going to picnic at Cottonwood Creek. The restaurant would be closed, and everyone was looking forward to the celebrations.

They'd no more than walked in the front door when Faith came hurrying out of the kitchen. "Oh, I thought you'd never get home. I have news."

"What kind of news?" Samantha asked as she and Ben followed his sister back to the kitchen.

Faith's eyes sparkled with excitement. "I found out for sure that there is a teaching position open. And they want it filled as soon as possible."

"Really?" Samantha grinned and dropped into a chair at the table while Ben took a seat next to her.

"What is this about?" he asked. "Samantha, were you a teacher back in Kansas?"

"Yes I was. I'm sorry I didn't mention it before. As I told Faith, with the school year in progress, I saw no need to apply."

"Well, no wonder you've been such a big help to Hope. We should have realized—"

"I had my suspicions," Faith said. "And when Hope's grades began to go up, I finally asked her."

"Then Faith said she'd heard a position would be open for the fall," Samantha added.

"But one is open now for the summer session. That's my news. Remember I told you one of the teachers was getting married?"

"Yes, but now?"

"She eloped last night. Seems she's. . .well. . .she's expecting a child, and she won't be able to hide the fact much longer."

"Oh!"

"Anyway, they need someone right away. Gabe built the principal's house, and he said that he'd like to come by and talk to you this evening, if that is all right with you."

"Why, of course." But now with Ben saying he'd like to court her, Samantha was wondering what she should do. He lived on a farm, after all. But they weren't courting yet. And what if he decided not to court her—decided that she wasn't the wife for him? She'd need to continue to make a living.

"Good. Because I asked Mr. Connors and his wife to join us for dinner."

"Oh!"

"Faith, maybe you should have waited to talk to Samantha—"

Samantha reached out and patted his forearm. "It's all right, Ben."

He looked down at Samantha with the sweetest expression. She was tempted to tell him he could start courting her at any time.

"As long as you are all right with it. This is wonderful news, though. You won't have to carry those heavy trays any longer."

"Oh, but I do hate to disappoint Mrs. Miller."

"She'll be happy for you, too, Samantha," Ben said. "She's come to care for you like a daughter."

"I know." She'd come to think of the older woman as a mother, too. And she loved talking to her. But she could still do that. And she could continue working on Saturdays for a while if Mrs. Miller needed help.

"I suppose I should go freshen up. Then I'll come back down and help."

"Don't worry about helping. You go get ready. I know he'll hire you right away. None of the teachers want to double up their classes, and he's certainly not going to want to teach. He's in more need than Mrs. Miller is right now."

"It'll be a lot easier on you," Ben said. "And me, too," he whispered when Faith turned to stir something on the stove. "I won't have to worry quite so much about all those single men asking to court you."

His smile had her heart doing double flips in her chest. It appeared Mrs. Miller was right. Her heart singing, Samantha smiled back before she hurried upstairs to get ready.

❧

Ben wasn't sure how he felt about the fact that Samantha had never told them she'd been a teacher. He wondered why she hadn't mentioned it, but it really wasn't any of their business. What was important was that they knew now, and she stood a good chance of getting a much better job.

"Something's different between you and Samantha today," Faith said. "What happened? Did you finally let her know how you feel about her?"

"And how might that be, sister of mine?" Ben decided to see what it was Faith believed she knew.

"Well, how about that you're in love with her?" Faith never was one to beat about the bush.

"So you are as observant as ever."

"I am. Have you told her?"

"Well, I haven't gone so far as to say the words. I'm not sure she's ready to hear them. But what tipped you off?"

"Ben, I've been your sister a long time. I know you. I can see the love in your eyes when you look at Samantha."

"Do you think she knows how much I care?"

"No." Faith shook her head. "At least not yet. But with men coming to the house, you might want to give her a hint."

"I have. I've told her that when she thinks she might want to start courting, I'd like to—"

"Oh Ben!" His sister's arms surrounded him. "I am so glad. She said yes, of course."

"Why 'of course'?"

"Because you are a wonderful man and she couldn't find a better one. And she's a wonderful woman. Hope and Matt love her, and well, she fits right into this family."

"I know. Say a prayer that it all works out, sis. She seems a little hesitant."

"You know I'll pray about it, Ben." Faith went back to the

stove and stirred her pot before turning back to him. "Maybe she's afraid she can't live up to Molly's memory."

"She doesn't have to."

"I know that and you know that, but you may have to convince her."

"Thanks, sis. I'll keep that in mind." Ben hadn't thought that Samantha might feel that way, might be afraid that he'd compare her to Molly. But they were two different women. His love for Molly had been part of him since he'd been a child. It was a warm and comforting love, and he thanked the good Lord that he'd had her.

But Samantha was—she made him feel things he'd never experienced before. With Molly, there'd been no reason to feel jealous of other men trying to court her because everyone knew they belonged together and no one tried to come between them. But Samantha was new in a town that had an abundance of men looking for a wife.

He'd never felt such anticipation in seeing Molly because he'd never gone a day without seeing her. But he couldn't wait to see Samantha after being away from her for days at a time.

He'd loved Molly with all his heart, and he'd never believed that their relationship lacked anything. But what he felt for Samantha was different—and maybe that was a good thing. They were two very different, very special women, and there would be no need to compare them. If that was something Samantha worried about, he would have to find a way to put her mind at rest.

❧

Samantha hurried back downstairs, hoping that she would make a good impression on the principal and his wife.

And she hoped that she'd see a happy couple so that she didn't have to worry about unwanted attention from another supervisor.

Her fears were set to rest as soon as she met Mr. Connors and his wife, Elaine. They were a younger couple and seemed to dote on each other. Both acted very excited that she would be able to start teaching the next week.

She showed Mr. Connors her teacher's certificate, thankful that it had been in the saddlebag she had been able to retrieve from the tent the day of the fire. He looked it over, and that seemed to be all he needed. He didn't ask where she'd taught before or for names of anyone to contact about previous employment.

"I can't believe how fortunate I am to be able to find a teacher at this late date," Mr. Connors said. "I was truly hoping that I wouldn't have to take the class over from now until the fall break. Thanks to you, Miss Carter, I won't have to. I'll contact the board and superintendent this weekend, but I am sure they will hire you on my recommendation. If you want the position, be ready to start on Monday morning. You'll be teaching the first- through third-grade classes."

"Thank you. I love that age group, and I look forward to teaching them."

Samantha kept expecting him to ask for references, but he didn't, and she breathed an inward sigh of relief when they left. Now that it was all settled, she was a little nervous.

"Oh, I hope I live up to his expectations," she said as the family gathered in the kitchen.

"And why wouldn't you?" Faith asked. "I've seen you help Hope. I have no doubt that you are a great teacher."

"And my grades have improved a lot," Hope added,

turning from the sink. "I wish you were teaching my class. Anyone would be very lucky to have you for a teacher, Miss Samantha. I'm glad you live here so I can still ask for your help." She paused, and a small frown furrowed her brow. "I can still do that, can't I?"

"Of course you can, Hope. And thank you for your encouragement. It's always a little nerve-racking to start a new job."

"You'll do fine," Ben said from where he leaned against the doorway leading into the dining room.

"Thank you, Ben. . .everyone. Now the really hard part comes. I have to tell Mrs. Miller I'm quitting tomorrow. I'm really not looking forward to that." She hoped that the woman who meant so much to her would understand and still be available to talk to.

"She'll be as happy for you as we are, Samantha," Faith said.

"And remember, if you don't like it or decide there's something else you want to do, you can always give your notice," Ben said. His eyes glittered as he looked at her, and Samantha wondered if he had something else in mind for her to do down the road. She hoped so.

ва

Ben walked to work with Sam the next morning to give her moral support when she told Mrs. Miller that she was quitting.

As he'd known she would, Mrs. Miller congratulated Sam on her new position.

"Samantha, dear, I am so happy for you. Had I known you were a teacher, I would have been working to get you hired myself. Guthrie needs all the good educators it can get, and I am thrilled you'll be teaching our children. But I'm not going to lie. I'm going to miss you."

Samantha looked as if she might cry, but then she regained her composure and hugged the older woman. "Thank you so much, Mrs. Miller. I'm going to miss you, too. But I'm not leaving Guthrie, and I will visit with you as often as I can. You've become very special to me and—"

"As have you to me. You're like a daughter to me, Samantha. You'd better come by often, or I'll be coming to find you."

"Oh, I will. I promise."

"Good. Now get on with you. You have a good day and celebrate your new teaching position."

"But I didn't mean to quit today. I'll work my regular hours. And if you need me on Saturdays for a while, I'll be glad to help."

"You don't need to do that, Samantha."

"I know. But I want to." She turned to Ben. "Thank you for coming with me. Will you see me home around two?"

"I'll be happy to." He'd be happy to do about anything for this woman. Seeing the admiring looks she got from nearly every man in the place, he was more than a little thankful that this was her last day working at the restaurant. Much as he hated the thought of leaving on Monday without finding out how Samantha's first day of teaching went, at least he could leave knowing she wouldn't be working here next week. That was a true blessing.

eleven

Independence Day dawned bright and sunny, and everyone was excited about the planned activities. Faith, Rose, and Samantha had been up since before dawn, frying chicken and making all kinds of good things to go with it. They'd baked pies and cakes the day before—most of the women were entering the baking contests.

Faith had let her boarders have the use of her oven the day before so they could enter the contests, too. Even Sam had baked a chocolate cake to enter.

"I don't expect to win, but with everyone else entering something, I got caught up in the excitement, too," she told Ben that morning.

With things getting busier at the farm, Ben had arrived in town late the night before, and although he'd been happy to hear that Samantha's first week of teaching had gone well, he really didn't have a chance to say more than a few words to her before it was time to call it a night. He was eager to spend the day with her and find out more.

The parade was going to take place that morning around ten, so breakfast was a hurried affair with everyone trying to get everything ready for the picnic to follow. That evening there would be fireworks down by Cottonwood Creek.

The plan was for everyone to walk to the parade and come back to pick up the food before heading over to the creek. As they took off for town, Ben made sure to walk with Sam.

"So, things went well this past week?"

"Yes. It was wonderful to be back teaching again. I didn't realize how much I'd missed it until I was back at it again."

Her smile lit the fire in his heart, and he wondered how long it would be before she agreed to let him court her. "I'm glad it went well."

"So am I. And it is much easier than working at Mrs. Miller's."

"Even with all those different-aged children?"

"Even with them." She smiled.

Ben was glad to hear it. All week he'd worried that she might wish she were back working at the restaurant. But now he found he worried that she might not be happy living out on the farm. He wished they were actually courting so he could find out about all kinds of things. But to ask outright. . . well, he wasn't quite ready to do that. Probably because he was afraid of what her answer might be.

By the time they got downtown, people were already lining the streets on both sides. Matt and Hope asked if they could join some friends on the other side of the street, and Ben gave his permission.

He looked down at Samantha and shrugged. "It's becoming more obvious to me that my children like living in Guthrie more than being out on the farm."

"Oh, I'm sure they want to be out there with you when they can—"

"No." Ben shook his head. "Oh, Matt doesn't seem to mind as long as it's for no more than a month or so at planting and harvesttime. He's mentioned that he's looking forward to harvest and even asked if he could bring a friend to help."

"Well, see?"

"I think he's torn. He loves helping Gabe, too. One day, he'll have to make a choice."

"And you know, by then he may decide on something entirely different. He's still young."

Ben nodded. "That's true. But Hope is definitely a city girl. She hasn't even mentioned coming out to the farm. I think she's afraid to tell me how she feels."

"You might make it easier and bring it up yourself."

"Maybe I will. I want them both to be happy, but. . ."

"You get lonely without them, I'm sure."

"I do. But as Faith has pointed out to me, they are growing up fast. And it was my choice to move out to the farm, not theirs."

"You could make them live with you."

"I could. But then it would take time out of my day and theirs for them to get to school and back. If I was going to do that, I should have done it from the first. Now it would seem selfish of me when I can come in on weekends most of the time." And even if they did live with him, it wouldn't be forever. What he needed was a wife. And the only woman he wanted to ask was the one standing beside him.

Ben knew it was because of Sam that he enjoyed the parade and the rest of the day immensely—because she was by his side. Everyone was happy when Rose and Faith tied for first place in the pie contest, and even though Sam lost the best cake contest, she didn't seem upset at all.

But when Ben took a bite of her cake, he leaned over to whisper, "You had it stolen from you. I can't imagine any cake better than this."

"Thank you, Ben. That means a lot to me—it was my mother's recipe."

They all enjoyed the picnic and the afternoon activities. But it was the fireworks that night that Ben would never forget. While the younger generation enjoyed the sparklers, he and Samantha shared a blanket with Gabe and Faith and watched the fireworks burst high overhead. As they *oohed* and *aahed* at each burst, Samantha's eyes shone with happiness. Ben hoped part of that was because they were sharing the evening together. The only thing better than this would be sharing their lives together.

But something was holding Samantha back from letting him know he could court her, and he had no idea what it was.

❧

Samantha enjoyed the whole weekend, especially going to church with Ben. She'd come to love their church family, and now she knew more of the members from teaching some of the children. It seemed to her that many of the people at church seemed to be looking at Ben and her as if they wondered if they were courting.

The long weekend passed by way too quickly, especially when, on Sunday evening, Ben announced that he wouldn't be able to get in to town every weekend for a while—at least not but for a night, here and there.

"Oh Papa, we'll miss you," Hope said. "I like having you in town."

"I know. And I like being here. But with the growing season upon us, I can't be asking Homer to watch over my crops and his every weekend. Besides his wife is back home now, and she might not appreciate it."

"Surely you can come in on Saturday nights, Ben," Rose said. "Most things can wait a day to be taken care of."

"I'll try, Rose. But that garden of yours sure can produce. And then there's the cane and the corn to see to."

"You know, I could ride out and help you on Friday evenings and be there to help you pick the produce and bring it in on Saturdays," Matt said.

"Thanks, son. I might need your help in another few weeks."

Samantha hated to see Ben leave on Monday morning. Something about seeing him leave alone had her wishing she could tell him she was ready to be courted, ready for him to propose marriage.

But fear that somehow her former principal would succeed in his threat to ruin her reputation had her hesitating—if that rumor followed her here, would Ben believe the lies or her? And since she hadn't told him, or even Faith, everything, would he decide she wasn't who he believed her to be?

She also worried that Ben wanted to court her only because he'd saved her life and somehow felt responsible for her. Samantha loved him with all her heart, and she wanted him to be happy. She owed him her very life. But he owed her nothing.

The next weekend Ben came in for supplies and to let them know that his neighbor Homer had sprained his ankle badly. "I'll be helping him out for a while," Ben explained. "It's the least I can do after all the times I've counted on him."

"Didn't you say his wife was back from her trip?" Rose asked.

"She is. But of course she can't take care of the farm all by herself. Hopefully Homer will be up and around in a few weeks, but for now, you probably won't see me except maybe

Saturday evening and part of Sundays. It'll depend on the workload."

The workload must have been heavy because Ben didn't make it in the next weekend. And Samantha found herself looking forward to the coming weekend even more than usual, hoping he'd be able to come into town. She missed Ben more each day and was glad to stay busy with settling into her new teaching job, planning lessons, and grading papers at night. She flew through the week on the anticipation that she might get to see Ben soon.

On Thursday she looked up from her desk to find Principal Connors knocking on her door with a woman and a young boy at his side.

"Miss Carter, I have a new student here for you. This is Jeffery Edwards and his mother."

"Miss Carter? Didn't you teach in Arkansas City?"

Dread flowed through Samantha. "Yes, I did."

"I thought so. You are the teacher who caused so much trouble for Mr. Jennings, aren't you?" The woman turned to Mr. Connors. "This woman will not be teaching my son. I'll put him in another school first."

Mr. Connors looked at Samantha questioningly. "Miss Carter? May I see you in my office? And Mrs. Edwards, won't you come tell us what this is all about?"

Samantha knew what it was all about. It appeared that Principal Jennings had kept his threat to ruin her reputation. She got one of the older children from the next class over to take charge and headed to Mr. Connors's office.

"Miss Carter, please take a seat, and we'll find out what this is all about."

"It's about this woman trying to seduce Mr. Jennings and

then blaming it on him! His wife even left him for it, and he's been fired—"

"That is not true, Mr. Connors." Samantha stood and looked the woman in the eye. "At least the part about me isn't true. I did not do this thing you are accusing me of, Mrs. Edwards."

"Well that's not what I heard." The woman stood and looked at Mr. Connors. "I'll be going to the school board about this first thing Monday. I won't have my son taught by the likes of her." She pointed a pudgy finger at Samantha.

"Please calm down, Mrs. Edwards. We'll get to the bottom of this matter, but—"

"You need to fire her immediately, sir!" The woman grabbed her son's hand and marched out of the principal's office.

Samantha was trembling so hard her legs felt wobbly. She dropped back into the chair and looked at Mr. Connors. "What she said is not true. But I can't prove anything, and it would be my word against his. I'm sorry, Mr. Connors, but before this gets out of hand and hurts anyone I care about, I must offer my resignation."

"Oh please, Miss Carter, don't act hastily. I don't want to accept your resignation. Let us get to the bottom of it all. If what Mrs. Edwards said is not true, you should fight her accusations."

"How do you fight rumors, Mr. Connors? Mr. Jennings threatened me in a most disgusting way. And it was only the arrival of my best friend, Annie Rogers, that stopped him from forcing me to—" Samantha couldn't finish the sentence. Didn't even want to think about it. "I gave him my resignation, knowing he would try to ruin my reputation.

Evidently he's convinced people to believe him, and how do I fight a lie?"

"You have people who would defend your honor, Miss Carter. What about this Annie person?"

Samantha shook her head. "I don't want her or anyone else hurt by all of this, don't you see? I don't want their reputations damaged because of being loyal to me. I can't let that happen. No, Mr. Connors. I'm resigning my position before anyone else I care about gets hurt—and before Mrs. Edwards can convince the school board to fire me."

❦

Samantha gathered up the personal items she had in her room and put them in the bag she'd brought them to school in. She tried to stay calm until the last bell and to hide how devastated she felt as she walked home with Matt and Hope.

Hope hurried upstairs to change her clothes and start her homework, while Matt went on to see if he could help Gabe down the street. Samantha wanted nothing more than to run to her room and hide under the covers, but she continued to the kitchen, knowing that if she didn't, Faith would guess something was wrong.

When she walked into the kitchen and Faith turned to ask how her day had gone, Samantha's resolve crumpled, and she dissolved into tears.

"Why Samantha, whatever is wrong?" Faith hurried to her side and enveloped her in her arms. "What's happened? Matt and Hope, are they—"

"They are fine. I'm sorry, Faith—I didn't meant to frighten you. It's. . .I. . ."

Rose seemed to appear from nowhere to set a cup of tea in

front of Samantha. "Drink this and tell us what's happened, dear."

Samantha managed to compose herself. Faith didn't need this kind of stress in her condition. "Thank you, Rose."

Both women made tea for themselves and sat down at the table. "Now, what is it that has you so upset? And what can we do to help?" Faith asked.

Samantha looked into her teacup and shook her head. "I don't think anyone can help. But what has happened is I've resigned my teaching position, and I am going to go to Oklahoma City and try to find work there."

"What!" Faith jumped up. "You'll do no such thing, Samantha Carter! What has happened to cause you to think like this? Have we done some—"

"No! Of course you haven't, Faith. Please, sit down and I'll try to explain." These people truly cared about her, and as much as she didn't want to have to tell them about what had happened, she really had no choice. She couldn't let them think they'd done anything to make her want to leave, nor could she leave knowing they'd hear the rumors and think they were true. She could only pray that they would believe her.

She explained the afternoon's events as quickly as possible. Then she looked at Faith and Rose and shook her head. "It's not true. I wouldn't even—"

"Of course it's not true. Why surely you never believed we would think it was?" Faith said. "That man—that principal Jennings—he's trying to save his own hide, isn't he?" Rose asked.

Sam nodded and began to sob. "He. . ." She haltingly explained what had happened up until the point where he threatened her.

"Did he. . .did he hurt you, Samantha?" Rose whispered.

"No." She shook her head. "The Lord was watching over me. Another teacher, a friend of mine, showed up just in time. I—I don't know what has happened since I left. I should have written her, but I didn't want him forcing her to tell him where I was or. . .give her any trouble."

"Oh, my dear." Rose had gotten up and come around to hug her. "You can't let this man win, dear."

"You can't leave us, Samantha," Faith said, wiping her eyes. "We love you. There's no need to—"

"Oh, but there is. I don't want your reputations to suffer because you took me in. I don't want your boardinghouse to get a bad name and—" The headache that had begun with Mrs. Edwards's accusations had become almost unbearable. "I feel I must leave. But I'm going to pray about it. Please don't worry if I don't come back down for supper, all right?"

"All right. You go get some rest. I'll check on you later."

"Thank you." Samantha got to her feet, but she couldn't leave the room until she hugged both women. "Thank you for believing me."

The very fact that they did had her hurrying out of the room and up the stairs before she started sobbing all over again. How could she leave this family she'd come to love? But how could she stay and bring trouble to them?

◦

Ben poured himself a cup of coffee and was thinking about heating up some of the beans and corn bread he'd made the night before when he heard a horse galloping up the lane to his house. He hurried outside to find Gabe swinging out of the saddle on his horse, Midnight.

His expression was grim, and Ben's heart seemed to drop

to his stomach. Something was wrong. "What is it, Gabe? What's happened? The kids? Sam—Faith? Are they all right?"

"They are all right. Well, as good as they can be with all that's happened. Samantha is having a tough time tonight, and yes, something has happened. Faith sent me to see if you can come into town before Samantha leaves."

"Leaves? What do you mean? Where is she going?" Ben was sure his heart had stopped beating.

"She says she's going to Oklahoma City to look for work," Gabe said.

"But she has a—"

"She gave her notice today. Pour me a cup of coffee, Ben, and I'll try to explain it best I can from what Faith and Rose told me."

Ben poured them coffee, and Gabe told him all he knew about what had happened in Kansas and what had happened that day to make Samantha quit her job. Ben found himself clenching and unclenching his fists over and over again. At once wanting to strangle the principal in Kansas and praying for forgiveness for even thinking of doing it. He'd never felt so much like harming another person in his life.

"He didn't—" He couldn't even finish the sentence.

"Samantha said no. She said the Lord was watching over her, and I'm sure He was because He sent another teacher to her room just in time to keep the man from harming her."

Thank You, Lord. Ben let out a huge sigh of relief. "But evidently he's carried through with his threat to try to ruin her."

"It appears that way. And she doesn't want to bring any trouble to any of us. That's why she wants to leave."

"Well, she's not going anywhere. Not if I have anything to

say about it," Ben said.

"You can come back with me?"

"I was coming in the morning anyway. Homer is better, and I've got crates of produce I need to bring in." And he'd been pining to see Samantha. "Everything is already loaded in the wagon. I'll be right behind you."

"Good. Faith said she'd keep supper warm for both of us. I'll see you back at home."

Ben quickly rinsed out their cups and the coffeepot, locked up, and hitched Rusty to the wagon. He saw no need to take the time to tell Homer he was leaving early.

Ben headed into Guthrie with a heavy heart that the woman he loved had been hurt not once but twice now by that low-life principal. He wasn't going to let it happen again.

twelve

All the way into Guthrie, Ben reviewed what Gabe had told him. No wonder Samantha hadn't been looking for a man. It could well be the reason she hadn't let him or anyone else court her.

He couldn't blame her, but oh, how he hoped to show her that not all men were like her former principal or the lawyer whose wife couldn't trust him to work with another woman. She had seen examples of true love in her own parents, in Gabe and Faith, and in other marriages right here in Guthrie. How was he going to convince her that he loved her? That he wanted to build a life with her?

Maybe she didn't care for him the same way he cared about her, but then she'd said she would let him know when she was ready to court. None of it made sense to him. Especially that she was thinking of leaving here when she'd made a place in this town for herself. She had true friends and people who cared for her, people who knew she wasn't the kind of woman to seduce a man. The idea was laughable. If she was the type of woman to chase after men, she'd had the opportunity to do that over and over again at Miller's Restaurant, but she hadn't. If she needed character references, she had a ton of them, and Ben was sure they'd all be willing to stand up for her, if needed.

But how was he going to convince her of that and get her to stay now, when she was afraid the rumors already spreading about her would follow her the rest of her life? She'd told Faith she didn't want to hurt their family. But if she went away, she'd leave an empty spot in his heart that could never be filled. Not only in his, but in his children's, Faith's and Gabe's, everyone who'd come to care for her. How did he get that across to her when she was determined to leave?

He couldn't let that happen. Ben reined Rusty into the yard between the office and the boardinghouse and tied him to the hitching post. He'd take him and the wagon to the stable at the back of the lot later. Right now he needed to see Samantha. Faith must have been on the lookout for him, because she slipped out of the back door and hurried to meet him.

"I checked on Samantha, and she's coming down to eat a bite. Says she doesn't want me stressing over her. But she doesn't know I sent Gabe to fetch you. I'll leave that up to you to tell her."

Ben could see the sheen of tears in his sister's eyes and knew she didn't want Samantha leaving either. He nodded. "I'll talk to her. I have no intention of letting her leave if there's anything I can do to stop her. Sis, you know that."

Faith nodded. "I do. Now might be the time to let her know how much you love her, you know?"

"I know. I'm not sure she'll believe it right now, though. But I can try. I'll do whatever I can to keep her here, Faith."

"Good, I feel better already. Come on in. I have supper in the warmer, and Gabe is hungry. I love that man. He didn't hesitate for one minute when I asked him to go get you. He kissed me and went to saddle Midnight."

"He knows how much Samantha means to all of us. And

you mean everything to him."

"I know."

Ben was glad to see the light back in his sister's eyes. He hoped he could keep it there. But he had a feeling that getting Samantha to see she needed to stay and fight wasn't going to be easy.

He followed Faith through the back door and was glad that Sam hadn't come down yet. He wanted to catch her by surprise and try to read how she felt about him being there.

"Papa!" Hope turned from the sink. "I was hoping you'd come in this weekend. I've missed you."

Ben hugged his daughter and kissed the top of her head. "I've missed you, too."

Right then, Matt came in the back door. "Papa, I'm glad you're here! I'd just gone over to the apartment when I heard the wagon come in the yard. It's good to see you."

"It's good to see you, too, son. It's been really hard not to get into town as often as I want. Thankfully, Homer is better, and I was able to take off."

Faith set plates down in front of Ben and Gabe when Samantha came into the kitchen.

"Oh! I didn't know everyone would still be here, I—Ben!"

She was surprised to be sure, and for a moment he could see that she was happy he was there. Then her mood seemed to shift, and her eyes filled with sadness. "I didn't know you were coming in tonight. And Gabe? Are you just now eating, too?"

"I am. Come join us."

If Samantha wondered why Gabe was only now eating she didn't ask, and Ben was glad. He wanted to talk about the situation with her in private. He only hoped his sister and brother-in-law would provide that opportunity for them after they finished eating.

❧

Samantha's heart couldn't hurt any worse if she'd been stabbed with a sharp knife. She didn't want to leave this man or his family. She didn't want to start all over anywhere. But she didn't want to bring them trouble of any kind. She had to leave—and the sooner the better.

While Ben and Gabe ate and talked, Faith served up the last of the pie she'd saved for them. In between the few bites Samantha managed to get down, she pushed the food around on her plate and tried to hide her loss of appetite. Why had Ben come in early? Did he know? No. There was no way—unless Faith sent Gabe to tell him. . . .

While Faith poured fresh coffee, Samantha handed her barely touched plate to Hope, praying that the girl wouldn't comment on her lack of appetite. Thankfully, Hope's attention was on her father, and she took the plate without commenting.

Samantha was about ready to head back upstairs but was afraid someone would ask if she was all right. She was afraid she would burst into tears if they did. She looked up to find Ben's gaze on her, and the warmth in his eyes was almost her undoing.

About that time Matt yawned, and Ben said, "Sounds like you're about ready for bed, son. Sorry I came in late and kept you up."

"I'm glad you're here, Papa. But I think I will head back to the apartment."

"We'll talk more tomorrow. I want to hear how things are going with you."

"All right." Matt yawned once more and headed for the door. "Good night, everyone."

"I think I'll go up, too," Hope said, sidling over to her father and putting an arm around his shoulders. She bent down and kissed his cheek. "I'm glad you're here, Papa."

"Me, too."

Once Hope went upstairs, it was as if a signal of some kind went off. Rose suddenly was exhausted, and Gabe forgot something at the office and asked Faith if she wanted to take a walk with him. Samantha found herself and Ben sitting alone at the table.

He lifted his cup to his lips and looked at her from over the rim. Then he set the cup down and asked, "Could I talk to you outside? No telling if someone will be coming back in here, and I'd like to talk to you in private."

Samantha couldn't think of what he needed to talk to her about that would make him sound and look so serious unless he somehow knew about today and—

"Sam?"

"Yes, of course you may."

"Let's go sit in the swing on the front porch. Not too many people come calling this time of night."

"All right."

Ben stood and pulled her chair out for her. "And let's go out the back door. That way we won't have the boarders wondering what we're up to if any of them are still in the parlor."

Samantha nodded and followed him out the back door. Lights from inside lit the way as they went up the porch steps and settled in the swing. Ben set it in motion with his boot and let out a deep sigh.

"What is it, Ben? What is wrong?"

He looked over at her and stopped the swing, propping his forearms on his knees. "Faith sent Gabe to the farm to tell me what happened earlier today. I'm so sorry, Sam."

Samantha wanted to be angry at Faith and Gabe for pulling Ben away from his work, for getting him involved, but she couldn't be. That they cared a great deal about her was evident by the man sitting beside her.

"I wish they hadn't pulled you away from your work just—"

"I'm glad they did. Sam, none of this is your fault. Anyone who knows you would never accuse you of seducing anyone. You aren't that kind of woman, and you shouldn't feel as if you have to run from a lie."

Samantha's heart swelled to near bursting as she realized that Ben didn't believe the lie. "But it will only get worse if I don't go, Ben. That woman was ready to spread what she'd heard far and wide. And if she believes the lie, other people will, too. I don't want your family hurt. I don't want Faith's business to suffer because of me."

"Samantha, we're all adults. None of us are afraid of some gossiping old biddy. People in this town know Gabe and Faith, and a lot of them have come to know you, too."

"But Ben, don't you see? It's still only my word against hers. . .or his. And Jennings could keep it going as long as he wants to. And then what if—" Samantha couldn't bring herself to say the words, but all she'd been thinking about for the past few hours was how those lies could hurt any children she might have one day. She wanted children, but how could she put them through that? How could she live with that fear hanging over her head?

"What if?" Ben asked. "What is it you are worried about?"

"I don't want those lies to hurt anyone I care about."

"But if everyone knows they are lies—"

"Lies can still hurt, even when one knows what they are, Ben." She shook her head.

"Gabe said you're planning on leaving. Is that right, Samantha?" Ben turned to her and lifted up her chin so he could look into her eyes. "Is it?"

"I don't know what else to do, Ben."

He sighed and ran a finger along her cheek. "You could stay here and let me court you. Better yet, you could marry me."

How could a heart flood with joy and sorrow all at the same time? Samantha loved Ben Thompson with all her heart, had loved him since the day he saved her life. And she would do anything for him except what she thought might hurt him. "Ben, I won't let you marry me only to save me from all these lies."

"That's not why I'd be marrying you, Samantha. I need a wife. I'm lonely."

He needed her. Her heart turned to mush. And who better to take care of him than someone who loved him as much as she did? Who better than someone who loved him with all her heart and who loved his children, too? But was that fair to him? Did he love her? Would he regret it one day? Could he love her the way she wanted to be loved? Or did he feel responsible for her because he had saved her life?

And even if they had no children together, what about *his* children, Matt and Hope? All this could hurt them, too. Her mind was in a whirl, and she knew now was not the time to make a decision. "Oh, Ben. I—thank you. You seem to always be there to come to my aide, to try to save me in some way. But I don't think I can let you do this. I—"

"Sam, I'm not asking you to make a decision right this minute. Please don't say no until you've had time to think about it and pray about it. Most important right now—don't leave town until we talk again. Please, promise me you won't."

Samantha was much too tired to argue with him, and she didn't really want to anyway. Besides she owed him so much. She couldn't turn him down.

"Sam?" His fingertip grazed her cheek again, taking her breath away. "Please don't do anything until we can talk more about this."

She gave a brief nod. "All right. You are right. We both need to think long and hard and pray about what I should do next. I won't leave until we've had time to do that."

Ben bent his head and grazed her cheek with his lips. "Thank you."

That did it. Samantha caught her breath on a sob. How could this man be so wonderful to her?

He tipped her face up, and his lips touched hers, softly, tenderly, before he leaned back, stood up, and pulled her to her feet and into his arms. "It's going to be all right, Sam. It is, I promise."

For one brief moment, she allowed herself to believe him.

thirteen

The moment Ben's lips touched Sam's, he knew he shouldn't have kissed her. Brief though the kiss was, he'd never forget the sweet warmth of her lips, and once would never be enough.

He wanted to talk long into the night, try his best to convince her to marry him, and kiss her again, but she looked so totally exhausted that he knew what she needed most was rest. They walked around back again, and he saw her inside the boardinghouse.

"Sleep well, Sam. Try not to worry. We're not going to let him ruin your life or ours."

"I'm not sure we can stop him, Ben. But thank you for being here for me, for coming in tonight."

"There is no place I'd rather be." And he meant it. He loved farming but not more than he loved this woman. He'd do anything he could to make her see they could have a good life together, that the Lord had brought them together for more reasons than just him keeping her from running back into that tent. "See you in the morning."

"All right."

"I trust that you'll be here."

"I promised. I will be."

"Sleep well, Sam."

"You, too."

Ben made sure she closed the door behind her and then forced himself to turn away and head across the yard. All the way, he prayed. *Dear Lord, please be with Sam tonight. Please give her peace and let her realize You are in control. Please give her comfort for the pain this man has caused her and help me to persuade her not to leave, not to let him have any control over her at all. Please help me to find a way to convince her of our need for her to stay here where she means so much to me and my family.*

Somehow Ben wasn't surprised to see his son waiting up for him when he opened the door to the apartment. Matt was drinking some hot chocolate that Faith had taught him to make in the same way Ben had taught her.

"There's more in the pan over on the stove, Papa. Want me to get you a cup?"

"I can get it, son. Thanks." Ben poured himself a cup and joined Matt at the table in front of the window. He could see no light in Samantha's room and wondered if she'd made herself a warm drink or if she'd run into Faith and Gabe. He took a sip of the sweet, warm drink. "You did good, Matt. This is real tasty."

"Thank you. Can you tell me what's going on, Papa?" Matt got right to the point. "Aunt Faith told me and Hope that she sent Uncle Gabe after you, that Miss Samantha needed you here. What's wrong? And why does Miss Samantha look so sad? She was fine this morning, but when school got out. . .well, she looked like she was about to cry even though she tried to act like everything was all right. But Hope and I knew something was wrong."

Ben needed no more proof that his children were maturing. If these rumors about Sam spread as fast as she seemed to think they might, he wouldn't be able to keep them from hearing about them. It would be much better coming from him.

"Well, son, we found out why Miss Samantha left Kansas to come here, and it's not a pretty story. But you and Hope are old enough to know what happened. That way, if you hear something, you can defend Sam more easily."

"What happened?"

"For starters, you know Samantha taught school up there, right?"

"Yes, sir. And she's a great teacher, too."

Ben nodded. He had no doubt about that. "Well, she had a principal who. . ." This wasn't going to be easy. He and Matt had talked about how to treat women, but—

"Who what, Papa?"

"He tried to get her to. . .become his mistress and threatened to ruin her name if she didn't. You know what her answer was. She resigned and left the state. But he meant what he'd said, and the lies have followed her here. He's saying she tried to seduce him."

Matt had just taken a sip of hot chocolate and spewed it all over the table. Ben quickly got a damp rag and wiped it up. Then he sat back down and continued. "The mother of a new student evidently believed the lies and told the principal here when they took her son to Samantha's class to introduce him as a new student. At the end of it all, rather than wait to be fired as Sam figured she would be, she gave her resignation."

"Oh, but she can't do that, Papa! She's a wonderful teacher, and she can't let lies—"

"I know, Matt. We've told her that. But she's afraid that they'll hurt all of us, and she thinks she has to move away to keep that from happening."

"Papa, you can't let her do that!"

"I know. I've asked her to stay here and marry me, but—"

"You did?" A grin split Matt's face before it turned to a frown. "And she said no?"

Ben shook his head. That gave him his biggest hope. She hadn't given him an outright no. "We've both agreed to think on it and pray on it. But at least she promised not to leave town until we talk about it again."

"Why do you think she didn't say yes right off? I'm sure she loves you, Papa. I've seen the way she looks at you."

Nothing his son could have said would have meant more to him at that moment. "I hope you are right, Matt. But again, I think she's putting us all first. She is afraid the rumors and lies will hurt us."

"They can't hurt us more than they've hurt her."

"I know that. It's convincing *her* that's the hard part."

"Maybe you ought to have Uncle Gabe talk to her. Remember how he was afraid that his being in jail for a crime he didn't commit would hurt Aunt Faith and any children they might have?"

Ben sat back in his chair and grinned at his son. "When did you get to be so smart, son?"

"I must take after you, Papa." Matt grinned back.

Ben chuckled. He was pretty sure his son was smarter. "Having your uncle talk to her is a great idea, son. I think I'll talk to Gabe about that. I may have to enlist the whole family's help to convince her she can't leave before all is said and done."

"You won't have to do any arm-twisting. We all want you and Miss Samantha to get together."

"Hope, too?"

"Yes. We've talked about it a lot."

His children never ceased to surprise him. They wanted him to marry again, wanted him to have someone to love. His heart swelled with love for them. "I think that might be something else she worries about. Being a stepmother and all."

"Well, she'd have nothing to worry about from us. We love her."

Ben swallowed hard. So did he. "I'll be calling on the two of you for help in the next few days, I'm sure."

"Anytime, Papa. Anytime."

Ben looked over across the way to see the light in Samantha's room was on. After talking to his son, Ben was sure he'd sleep better. He prayed that Samantha would sleep well, too. It was going to be all right. He would put his trust in the Lord and count on Him and the family he'd been blessed with to make it so.

ঌ

Samantha thought Faith and Gabe had gone to bed when she came back inside, but as soon as she locked the back door and turned around, it was to find them at the kitchen table as if they were waiting for her. "Oh, I'm sorry! I thought you'd already retired for the evening."

Gabe chuckled. "We were waiting up for you."

"We wanted to make sure you are all right before we went to bed."

Tears gathered in Samantha's eyes once more at the love these people showed her. "I'll be all right. But I hate for any of this to touch you—you've all been so good to me."

"Please, come sit with us, Samantha," Faith said. "I have a pot of hot chocolate. Would you like some? It might help you sleep better." She jumped up to pour a cup before Samantha answered.

"That would be nice. Thank you, Faith." Samantha took a seat at the table. The aroma from the cup Faith handed her took her back to her childhood when her mother would make hot chocolate whenever she was feeling blue. She closed her eyes and took a sip. "Mmm. This is wonderful."

"I know it's the wrong time of year for it, but I love it anytime. It's a—"

"Drink of comfort."

"Yes. I hope so, anyway. We're so sorry about the day you've had and—"

"Thank you for believing me, for trying to help and for sending for Ben. I still think I should leave, but I've promised him I won't do anything until we talk again."

"Good. I'm glad to hear it."

"I don't want all of this to hurt any of you."

"Samantha, you are the one who's been hurt. We're sitting here wanting to make things right for you, and you're worried about bringing trouble to us," Gabe said. He and Faith exchanged a look, and his wife gave a slight nod.

"You know, you aren't the only one who has something in their past they'd rather not think about again. Something they'd rather the whole town not know about," Gabe said.

A shadow of sadness passed over his eyes as he stopped to take a sip of hot chocolate. But then he looked at Faith and smiled, and Samantha could almost feel the love arcing between them. He took his wife's hand and turned his attention back to Samantha.

"I was engaged before. Several years ago, my fiancée begged me to sell out and go back to Virginia, but I wanted to hold on. Then when she was in town one day, a bank robber shot and killed her." He paused and took a sip from his cup, then cleared his throat. "After that, all that mattered to me was finding the man who shot her. For a year, I hunted him down. Going from lead to lead and town to town."

Samantha's heart went out to him at the loss of his fiancée and the misery that must have followed as he sought to avenge her death. She swallowed around the lump in her throat as she saw the tears that shimmered in Faith's eyes as she heard her husband recount those years before they met.

"When I caught up with him, all I wanted was to take him in, but the man shot at me, and"—Gabe let out a deep breath and rubbed the bridge of his nose—"I shot back, wounding him but not killing him. I took him in, but that wasn't the end of it. He claimed to be innocent, and we were both put in jail until the sheriff could get to the truth. I was there several months until a trial proved that the man was the robber and my fiancée's assassin. I was never so glad to get out of Kansas in my life."

"And then we met," Faith said. "After my husband died, I believed I'd never be able to have children and had decided never to marry again. And Gabe was— "

"I was afraid that my past would come back to haunt me and anyone I might love, especially any children I might have one day."

Faith smiled and wrapped her arms around her middle. "I suppose we'll find out about all that later. But what we've decided to do is face it head-on. Tell this child and any others we might have about it. After all, Gabe only shot the man in self-defense. But if they know about it and some-one brings it all up later, it won't have the power to hurt them like it would if we tried to keep everything a secret."

They were absolutely right. Samantha knew they were. And what Gabe had gone through was heartbreaking and in so many ways much worse than what she was dealing with. Still, the other man had killed his fiancée, and no one was going to blame Gabe for trying to find him.

Even though it was worse, it still wasn't quite like a woman's reputation being sullied. That kind of rumor would have people always wondering if it was true. And it was her word against Jennings's. Some people believed his lies without even asking her if they were true. But it couldn't have been easy for Gabe and Faith to go over all their heartaches again for her sake. "Thank you for sharing your past with me, both of you. I am so happy you two found each other."

"You can have the same kind of life, Samantha. Please, think it over and pray about it. We don't want you to go."

"And I don't want to leave. But I'm not sure I can stay. . . ." How did she say that she didn't want Ben to marry her just to save her again? She wanted his love. "But I did promise Ben, and I promise you, that I won't be going anywhere until we talk again."

"Then that will be good enough for us," Gabe said.

Samantha hoped so. Because it was all she could give at the moment. "I think I'll turn in now, but I'll see you both in the morning." She didn't want them worrying that she would leave in the middle of the night.

"See you then. I hope you rest well," Faith said.

"Thank you both again for sharing something that I know wasn't easy for you."

Gabe smiled. "It'll be worth it if you decide to stay."

Samantha smiled and headed upstairs. What a blessing to

have people in her life who cared so much about her. How could she bring trouble to them? Yet how could she bear to leave? She was glad it was quiet upstairs. She didn't think she could talk to anyone else tonight, and she couldn't wait to crawl beneath the covers and sink into her bed.

Revived a bit by the time she readied herself for bed, she looked out her window at the apartment across the way. Lights were still on, and she could see Ben and Matt at the kitchen table. Oh, how she loved that man. She wanted nothing more than to tell him she would marry him, but she had much more to think about than simply what *she* wanted.

He had two wonderful children to consider. She didn't want to bring them any embarrassment. And as for Ben, she had no doubt he'd defend her honor until the day she died, but was she what he needed? How could she bring honor to his name with rumors swirling about them at any time? She turned away from the window and went to turn her bed down. Then she slid to her knees and prayed.

"Dear Father, please help me to know what I should do," she whispered. "Please help me to do what is best for Ben and his children, for Faith and Gabe. I don't want to bring any embarrassment or sorrow of any kind to them. And I don't want to leave them. I love them all. Please help me to know what to do. And if it is to stay, then please help me to be strong enough to withstand the rumors around town, the looks and the whispers behind my back that I'm sure to encounter. Thank You for these people You've placed into my life. Help me to do what is right for them. In Jesus' name, I pray. Amen."

A lone tear slipped down her cheek as she finished her

prayer, pushed herself up, and slipped beneath her covers. But for the first time since that afternoon, she felt at peace, knowing that the Lord would guide her. In His time.

fourteen

At around eight the next morning, a knock on the door startled Samantha awake. For a moment she thought she'd overslept and was going to be late for school, but then she remembered that she'd given her resignation. Remembering why gave her a heavy heart as the knock sounded once more.

"Yes? Who's there?"

"It's Rose, Samantha. May I come in?"

"Of course, Rose. One minute." Samantha slipped on her wrapper and hurried to unlock the door. Rose stood with a big tray holding a pot of tea, two cups, and a plate of toast in her hands.

"Oh Rose, you didn't have to—"

"I know. But we were all starting to worry when you didn't come down at your regular time, and I wanted to have my say before you do anything today. May I join you for tea?"

"Of course you may." Samantha held the door open wide for her to come in.

Rose set the tray on the table by the window and pulled up an extra chair from the writing desk. Samantha took a seat as the older woman poured them each a cup of tea.

"I had a feeling you might be feeling a bit sick at your stomach after all the goings-on yesterday," Rose said. "The toast might help."

Sam couldn't even remember if Rose had been there when she'd told Faith what had happened, but evidently she knew.

And obviously, she was trying to help in her own way. Well, at least she wouldn't have to tell the whole story again.

Rose took a seat and held out the plate of toast. She was right. Samantha's stomach didn't much take to the smell of bacon and eggs that had followed Rose up the stairs. Toast might be the only thing she'd be able to keep down. She took a piece and bit in, chewing slowly as Rose began to speak.

"Now, I came to say a few things, and even though I know it's really none of my business what you do, I care a great deal about what you decide. First off, no one who knows you is going to believe you seduced that principal up in Kansas. Not that you couldn't, mind you—but that you wouldn't."

"Thank you, Rose."

Rose gave a short nod and continued. "Second is that this whole family loves you, Samantha. Like me, you've become like family to them. Fact is, none of us wants you to leave. If you are worried about any rumors embarrassing us or causing us trouble, put that right out of your mind. We can handle it."

"Oh, Rose. . .I don't know what to say."

"It's all right. You don't need to say anything. But I'm not finished yet." She grinned. "I have more to say."

Samantha couldn't contain a giggle. "All right, Rose. You let me know when you are through."

"Well, there's Ben. He's a right special man."

"Yes, ma'am, he is."

Rose gave a short nod. "Well, he was one of the lonesomest men I've ever known, until you came into his life."

Rose had all her attention now, and Samantha waited for her to continue.

"You've given him someone to care about besides his children—to dream of a future with. Matt and Hope love him, but they don't want to live his life. They are dreaming of their own futures. It's not going to be all that long before they find mates of their own. Ben needs someone to share his life with now and later."

"But I'm not sure I—"

"You are afraid you won't measure up to his Molly, aren't you?"

Samantha sighed. "He loved her very much, and from all accounts she was a near-perfect wife. There's nothing perfect about me, Rose."

"There's nothing perfect about any of us, Samantha. Not even Molly. I'm sure she was a wonderful woman, but the reason she is held in such high esteem is because she loved them all, probably with everything she was. You love them, too. I can see it in your eyes and hear it in your voice when you speak to them—especially Ben. My question to you is, do you love them enough to stay here and show them how much you care?"

"But Rose, I don't want to bring them any—"

"Sorrow? Trouble? Pain? Don't you know that if you leave, you'll bring them—us—all of those things? And you will always wonder if you've done the right thing. Don't have any regrets, Samantha. Stay here and live life abundantly, the way the Lord wants you to. Give it all over to Him, and let Him take care of it. Be still and listen to Him."

With that, Rose got up, gave Samantha a hug, and left the room. Samantha sat speechless. What could she say to all of that? Except that maybe it was time she did as Rose suggested. Be still and listen.

❧

"Well? Is she all right? Did she say what she is going to do?" Ben asked when Rose came back downstairs.

"No. But she's not packing to go anywhere yet. I don't know if anything I said will change her mind, but I tried, Ben."

"Thank you, Rose." He exhaled deeply and looked at Faith and Gabe. They'd told him about their conversation with Samantha the night before. "And thank you for telling her your story, Gabe. You've all done what you can, and I appreciate it. Now I guess it's up to the good Lord to keep her here."

A knock on the front door had Faith hurrying down the hall to answer. But Ben and Gabe were both on their feet as they heard her say, "Mr. Connors, Mrs. Connors, what brings you here this morning?"

"I'd like to speak to Miss Carter, if I may," Mr. Connors said.

By then Ben was at his sister's side, and Gabe stood right behind her.

"I'm not sure she—"

"Please, Mrs. Logan. My husband doesn't wish to hurt Miss Carter. We've talked things over, and we're here to help, if we can."

Faith looked at Ben. He nodded. Anyone who was trying to help keep Sam here was more than welcome to try.

"I'll go see if I can get her to come down," Faith said.

"Thank you."

"Why don't you wait in the parlor? The boarders have come down for breakfast and—"

"Of course," Mr. Connors said. "We don't want to disturb them."

Faith turned and hurried up the stairs while Gabe and Ben showed the principal and his wife into the parlor.

"Please take a seat. They'll be back down soon."

Ben hoped that was the case. It was possible that Samantha would refuse to come down. But if these people truly wanted to help her, he hoped she'd talk to them. Whatever they had to say, they were going to say it in front of him. He wasn't leaving Samantha to deal with any more heartache alone.

❧

Samantha had been trying to do as Rose suggested. She'd sat still with her eyes closed and held her Bible, asking the Lord to let her know what she should do. The peace that settled over her while remembering some of her favorite verses about the Lord never leaving her assured her that He was there with her, that He always was. She had only to give her worries over to Him.

But running footsteps down the hall and a knock on her door startled her out of her peaceful state. She hurried to open the door and found Faith. "Samantha, Mr. Connors is here to see you. He says it's very important that he talk to you, and even his wife is with him."

"Oh Faith, please—" No, she couldn't do that. It wasn't right to ask Faith to make excuses for her. She had to handle this herself—no, she had to look to the Lord to help her handle it. "Tell Mr. Connors that I'll be right down."

"You don't have to talk to them alone. Ben and Gabe and I will be there."

"Thank you. I'll hurry."

Samantha dressed quickly and arranged her hair on top of her head. She looked a little pale and pinched her cheeks to give them some color before heading downstairs. Mr. and Mrs. Connors waited in the parlor with Ben, Gabe, and Faith.

Mr. Connors stood when Samantha entered the room. "Miss Carter, thank you for seeing us. I realize that yesterday must have been very hard on you. I wanted to let you know about some new developments."

"New developments?" Samantha looked from Mr. Connors to Ben, who'd come to stand beside her, and back again. "What are you talking about, Mr. Connors?"

"Why don't we all go into the kitchen?" Faith suggested. "I know it's not very formal, but the boarders usually use this room after breakfast, and they'll be through anytime now."

"Thank you, Faith. Yes please, if you don't mind, Mr. and Mrs. Connors, let's go to the kitchen."

Faith led the way, and Samantha followed with Ben and Gabe right behind her.

"Do you want us to leave?" Gabe asked Samantha.

"I'm not going anywhere," Ben said. "Samantha needs our support, and I'm not leaving her here to deal with this alone." He looked firmly at Mr. Connors, and Samantha's heart swelled with love for the man who always seemed to put her first.

"That is up to you, Miss Carter," Mr. Connors said. "I certainly don't mind if they stay. It might not be a bad idea."

"Please, everyone take a seat. Would you like some coffee or tea?" Faith said without waiting for Samantha's answer. It was as if they'd all made up her mind for her, and she had to smile. She took a seat beside Ben, and when he held out his calloused hand to her, she took it. It comforted her to know he was there for her.

"We're fine, Mrs. Logan, thank you," Mrs. Connors said. "I insisted on coming with my husband because I want Miss Carter to know that we both are supporters of hers and. . .I suppose I should let him tell Miss Carter what's happened."

"Thank you, dear," Mr. Connors said with a loving look directed at his wife. He turned back to Samantha. "After you left yesterday, the superintendent came over to speak to me. It seems Mrs. Edwards beelined it to his office."

"That doesn't surprise me, Mr. Connors, and it's not really a new development. I figured she'd be talking to him and the school board, too, for that matter."

"I understand. But what happened right after that is the news."

"Oh? And what would that be?"

"Your old principal came asking about openings for a principal at any of the schools."

"Mr. Jennings? Here in Guthrie?" Samantha sat up straight.

"Yes, ma'am. Apparently he is no longer working in Kansas. Said he wanted to come to Guthrie and be in on starting a new school system here."

"Then what Mrs. Edwards said about him being fired— that must be true."

"I think it is."

"But, you aren't leaving, are you, Mr. Connors?"

"No. I'm staying right here. But there is an opening for a principal coming up at Vilas Avenue, and the school board put an advertisement in the paper about a week ago. Somehow he'd gotten word of that."

"He can't get hired here, Mr. Connors." Suddenly, Samantha knew what she had to do. "If he's hired here, he might try to do the same thing with another teacher that he tried to do with me. We can't let him do that, Mr. Connors."

"I was hoping you'd say that. Even the superintendent

wondered about him. Did you go to the school board in Kansas about him?"

"No." Samantha shook her head. "He'd already threatened that he would ruin my reputation if I didn't give in to his demands. I had no intention of doing that, but I didn't think anyone would believe me. So I left."

"I wondered if something like that might have happened. Somehow, someone else must have gone to his wife or the school board if he was fired. It's possible he found out you were here and followed you."

Samantha drew in a sharp breath and shook her head. "I don't know how he'd know. I haven't even written my best friend, Annie Rogers, because I didn't want her to have to lie to him."

"He's not going to get to you, Samantha. I promise you that," Ben said.

She took comfort from his words and the squeeze he gave her fingers.

"Well, I might have to ask you to face him one more time," Mr. Connors said. "There is an emergency school board meeting tonight. He'll be there, and I was hoping—"

It was as if everyone around the table held their breath waiting for Samantha to say something. She shuddered inwardly at the thought of seeing Jennings again, but she knew she had to go. She couldn't let him get away with treating another teacher like he had her. She wouldn't be facing him alone. Ben would be by her side, as would Faith and Gabe, probably Rose, too. But most important of all, the Lord would be with her, and she was ready to hand the situation over to Him.

"What time?"

"The meeting is at seven o'clock."

Samantha let out a big breath and smiled. "There is no way I can let Jennings get into this school system. I'll do all I can to keep him from treating anyone here the way he treated me. I'll be there."

"We'll all be there," Ben said. "Hope you've got a room big enough."

Mr. Connors looked at him. "It's big enough to bring as many people as you want."

Ben nodded and grinned. "Good."

Somehow, that smile put her fears to rest—well, that and knowing the Lord would be there with them.

fifteen

When Mr. and Mrs. Connors took their leave, promising to be at the meeting before Samantha arrived, a flurry of activity erupted.

"Let's go shopping," Faith said. "You need all the confidence you can get, and while my old clothes worked well for a while, you need something nicer for tonight."

"Oh, I don't know—"

"Yes. I'll put a roast in the oven for dinner, and it can cook all day."

"I'll fix lunch for the ladies, and you won't have to worry about that," Rose offered.

"Oh, I don't know, Faith," Samantha said again. "The things you gave me are plenty nice enough—"

"No, they aren't. I don't get in the mood to go shopping often, Samantha. And I could use a few things. Everything is getting too tight for me and—"

"And she'd like some company," Gabe said, his arm around his wife.

"Oh! Well, I'll be glad to go shopping with you, Faith. Let me go get my reticule and hat, and I'll be ready to go."

"Good. I'll get the roast in the oven."

Once Samantha was out of earshot, Ben hugged his sister. "Thank you. She needs to get out and do something. She'll get more nervous by the hour about that meeting tonight if she doesn't have something to do."

"I agree. But I told the truth. I can use a few new things. I'm hoping that since she's staying to fight, she's changed her mind about leaving. But right now I only want us to get her through tonight." Faith seasoned the roast and seared it in a dutch oven while she was talking.

"So do I," Ben said. He wasn't sure what had happened since he'd talked to Samantha last night, and now didn't seem the time to question her. But he couldn't be happier that she was going to stay at least long enough to fight Jennings at the school board meeting. For now, he only wanted to support her. And he had an idea of how to go about it.

Faith added water to the dutch oven, but before she could pick it up to put in the oven, her husband grabbed it and did it for her. Then he kissed the tip of her nose and said, "I guess I'd better get to work. You buy anything you need, you hear?"

"I will." Faith stood on tiptoe to kiss him.

Ben tamped down a surge of envy at seeing them so close when he was afraid he might lose Samantha forever. He had to do what he could to see that they had a chance for a future together. "I have some errands to run. I'll be back in plenty of time before the meeting, though."

"I know you will. I'm going to get ready." Faith turned to Rose. "Thank you for offering to take care of lunch for me."

"You're welcome. I'll add the vegetables to the roast a little later. You enjoy the day. It's about time you took a few hours for yourself."

"Thank you, Rose."

Ben and Gabe headed out the door at the same time.

"I have a feeling you're planning something to help Samantha tonight. Need any help?" Gabe asked.

"I do have a plan, but I don't want to take you away from your work," Ben said.

"I can check on how the work is going. If you need help, come with me; then I'll help in any way I can."

"All right. Let's go."

&

Samantha had never been so nervous in her life. She hadn't been able to eat a bite of dinner, and now as she and Ben, Faith, and Gabe made their way to the school board meeting, she almost wished she hadn't agreed to go. But she couldn't let Jennings get by with treating any other teacher as he had her. She wasn't bent on revenge—she would have been happy never to have had to see the man again—but the school board needed to know what kind of man he was.

He'd told lies about her, and she couldn't let them stand without telling the truth about what had happened. If the school board didn't believe her, then she would know she'd done her best. That she hadn't run away this time.

They were early, but she was glad to see that Mr. and Mrs. Connors were waiting for them.

"I'm so glad you came," Mr. Connors said.

"He's been afraid you might not show up." His wife smiled at Samantha as she put a hand on her husband's arm. "He really wants you back teaching, Miss Carter. The parents of all the children you've taught have told him how much better their children are doing since you began teaching them."

"Good educators are not easy to find, Miss Carter. That's why I told the superintendent that I didn't want to accept your resignation—that and the fact that from the beginning I doubted Mrs. Edwards was telling the truth about what happened."

"I almost backed out," Samantha said. "But. . ." She shook her head. "I can't let him get hired here. I can't."

Mr. and Mrs. Connors led them up to a small room to the side of the bigger room. "I decided it might be best if Jennings—or Mrs. Edwards, for that matter—can't see you until we call on you. We'll let them have their say and then bring you in. The superintendent knows what I've planned, and he's looked into a few matters also. I think everything is going to work out fine, but know this, Miss Carter. No matter what happens tonight, neither my wife nor I think for one moment that what Mrs. Edwards said about you and Jennings is true."

"Thank you, I appreciate your letting me know that," Samantha said. She turned to Ben and Faith and Gabe. "You all don't need to stay with me. I'll be fine here. I promise, I won't bolt."

"I'm not going anywhere, Samantha," Ben said, "but Faith and Gabe can go out and listen for us."

"They can sit with us," Mrs. Connors said. "We don't want to take a chance of that Jennings person seeing you and figuring out what we intend to do."

"I'm not even sure what it is you are expecting of me," Samantha said.

"Well, I'm not sure exactly how things will proceed, but Mrs. Edwards has asked to talk to the board about you. I'm not even sure she knows Jennings is going to be here. It should be interesting, to say the least. But once she's said her spiel and Jennings is introduced and questioned, I think that would be a good time for you to be introduced and tell your story. I hope that will be acceptable to you, Miss Carter?"

"I believe so."

"All right. Then we'll go out to the meeting. I believe you'll be able to hear the proceedings from here, but I will come and get you when the time comes."

"I'll be here."

She watched as Gabe and Faith followed Mr. and Mrs. Connors out of the room. True to his word, Ben stayed put. But he turned to her as soon as the door closed. "Are you sure you are all right, Sam? I want you to fight for yourself, but I—"

"I'm fine with anything that will let the truth about Jennings come out, Ben. I don't look forward to it, but after a lot of soul-searching and trying to listen to the Lord, I've decided that I can't run from Jennings's lies for the rest of my life."

"Thank You, Lord," Ben whispered. He reached out and pushed an errant curl behind her ear. "I'm glad you listened to Him, Sam."

Samantha smiled at him. "So am I."

"Does this mean that—"

The sound of a gavel hitting hard against a table interrupted Ben, and they both hurried over to the door to listen. Ben cracked open the door, and although they couldn't see the table where the board sat, they were able to glimpse the end of the first row where Mr. and Mrs. Connors sat. Faith and Gabe were in the next two seats.

Samantha and Ben moved so that they couldn't be seen and tried to hear what was going on, but the room seemed quite full and the noise level was high, so most of what they heard was a bit garbled. Several times, they heard the gavel bang and someone say, "This meeting will come to order!"

Each time, they moved a little closer to the door, still

unable to make sense out of anything being said. It seemed to go on forever as they strained to hear what was being said—to no avail.

"I can't understand a thing they are saying." Ben's husky whisper warmed her ear, making Samantha aware of how very close they were standing.

Her eyes met his, and her heart fluttered as he lowered his head to hear her reply.

"Neither can I," she breathed, her heart pounding so hard it was the only thing she could hear. No wonder the conversation in the other room faded into the background.

Samantha held her breath as Ben reached out, tipped her chin up, and looked down into her eyes. "Sam, have you decided to—I mean, are you—"

The doorknob turned, and Ben gently pushed her away from the door as quickly as he could before Mr. Connors stepped inside.

"Miss Carter, could you step into the meeting room? I believe several people will be surprised to see you. But before you go, I must tell you that Mrs. Edwards spoke to the board, asking that they accept your resignation, and Mr. Jennings has said he was fired because you accused him of making unwanted advances, when it was you who—"

"That's not true at all!"

"Yes, I know. I just wanted you to be aware of what has already been said about you. But now it is time to have your say, and I'm glad to tell you that you have plenty of supporters in the room, so there is no need to feel nervous. Tell the truth, and the Lord will take care of the rest."

Samantha inhaled deeply and nodded. She had to trust the Lord. She had no control over what the board would believe.

She'd do what she could and leave the outcome in the Lord's hands.

"Ready?" Mr. Connors asked

"As ready as I'll ever be, I suppose." She looked at Ben. He gave a slight nod and grasped her elbow. They let Mr. Connors lead the way.

❧

Samantha tried to keep her mind on the task at hand, but she couldn't keep from looking out into the crowded room. In the front row on the other side of the room sat Mrs. Edwards and Principal Jennings, both wearing surprised expressions. Ben took a seat beside Gabe, and Mr. Connors showed her to a seat at the side of the table the board was seated at.

The president of the board welcomed her. "Miss Carter, I am glad you could join us tonight. We've heard some rather unsettling information, and we believe you can clear things up for us, if you will be so kind as to answer a few questions."

"I'll be glad to answer to the best of my ability, sir."

"Good. Do you by any chance know the two people sitting over there? Mrs. Edwards in the green dress and Mr. Jennings next to her?"

"I know who they are. I only met Mrs. Edwards the other day when she came to enroll her son in school. But once she saw me, she leveled untrue accusations at me and said I couldn't teach her son."

"She's lying!" Mrs. Edwards yelled. "I spoke the truth."

"You had your say, Mrs. Edwards. It's time to hear from Miss Carter now," the president said before turning back to Samantha. "And Mr. Jennings? Do you know him?"

"Yes, sir. He was the principal at the school where I taught before I came here to Guthrie."

"And why did you leave that school, Miss Carter?"

Dear Lord, give me courage. She let out a deep breath. "I left because Mr. Jennings was making unwanted advances to me, and when I wouldn't give in to them, he threatened to ruin my reputation. The day I left, he caught me alone in my classroom, and if not for one of the other teachers walking in. . ."

Samantha shuddered and shook her head before turning to the board. "Whether or not you accept my resignation—I gave it because I didn't think I could fight Mrs. Edwards's rumors—knowing what kind of man he is. But I cannot stand by and let you hire Principal Jennings. I don't want him to have the opportunity to do to another teacher what he tried to do to me. You need to know what kind of man he is."

Jennings jumped up from his seat. "I can hear no more. This woman is lying! It was she who came after me and—"

The gavel banged down on the table. "Order here! Sit back down, Mr. Jennings. I believe we can get to the truth of the matter quite soon. Mr. Connors, will you bring in the supporting witness for Miss Carter?"

Samantha looked from one man to the other and then to Ben. She had no idea whom they were talking about.

"I will." Mr. Connors crossed the meeting room, walking right in front of Jennings and Mrs. Edwards, to the doorway of another room straight across from the one Samantha and Ben had been in. A moment later, Mr. Connors was back with. . .

Samantha caught her breath and smiled. It was Annie Rogers. Annie caught her eye and grinned.

"This is Miss Annie Rogers, the friend and teacher Miss

Carter mentioned. She didn't know we contacted Miss Rogers as soon as we heard about her. Annie was more than happy to come tell us about what she knows about Mr. Jennings."

"Miss Rogers, thank you for coming. Please take a seat."

Mr. Connors showed her to the seat Samantha had just vacated.

Annie looked at Samantha and smiled, and Samantha had no doubt that the Lord was going to see that justice was done.

"Miss Rogers, we've been told several conflicting stories tonight, and we're hoping you can shed some light on things for us."

"I'll certainly try to," Annie said.

"Can you tell us anything you know about what happened between Mr. Jennings and Miss Carter that would have made her resign her teaching position at the school where you both taught?"

"I can." Annie looked Jennings in the eye—until he looked away. "I knew he'd been making suggestive remarks to Samantha for some time. He'd been implying that he cared for her and that. . .well, that he wanted a relationship with her."

"And what did Miss Carter say about all of that?"

"She ignored as much of it as she could. But then the day that she resigned, he threatened to ruin her reputation if she didn't. . .didn't go along with what he wanted. He even cornered her in her classroom."

"How do you know this?"

"Because I walked in right as he reached her, and she began to raise a small gavel from behind her back to defend herself."

A collective gasp rose among the onlookers.

"That's not true either!" Jennings shouted.

"Oh but I'm sure it is!"

Samantha heard Mrs. Miller's voice yell out, and she turned to see her former employer come forward.

"Mrs. Miller, you have something you'd like to say?" the president asked.

"I do." She didn't bother to take a seat, addressing the board from her feet. "Miss Carter worked for me before she took the teaching position here in Guthrie. A nicer, more moral woman I've never employed. And I've got a ton of witnesses to the fact that she never gave any man reason to think that she would respond to any advances they might want to make, much less make any kind of advance toward them." She turned to the onlookers. "Those of you who can vouch for the character and morals of Miss Carter, please stand up."

Samantha turned to see almost all of the men she'd ever waited on at the restaurant stand, hat in hand. One at a time they spoke, telling how they'd tried to get her to let them walk her home, court her, or accept their proposals of marriage, and they all had the same response, a sweet "No, thank you," from Miss Carter.

By the time they were through, both Jennings and Mrs. Edwards were squirming in their seats.

"Thank you, gentlemen," the board president said before turning to Annie, who was still seated near the board members. "Miss Rogers, do you know the woman named Mrs. Edwards?"

"I do. She is a cousin of Mr. Jennings, I believe."

"Is that true, Mrs. Edwards?"

"What if it is?" Mrs. Edwards huffed. "It doesn't change the facts."

"No, I suppose it does not. The board and I will adjourn for a few moments, and we will let you know what we have decided in regard to Miss Carter's resignation, Mr. Jennings's employment in this town, and Mrs. Edwards's complaint against Miss Carter."

They filed out of the room, and Samantha hurried over to Annie and gave her a hug. "However did you know I needed you?"

"Mr. Connors telegraphed the school yesterday, and they had me telegraph him back. He said you needed help tonight and could I come? Of course I said yes. He even bought my train ticket."

"Oh thank you, Annie. You are a sight for sore eyes! I've missed you but didn't want Jennings to try to force my whereabouts from you."

"It's all right. I understand. I'm so glad to be in contact again, though."

Samantha introduced her friend to Ben, Faith, and Gabe, but before they could thank Annie for coming to Sam's aid, the board walked back into the room.

Annie took a seat beside Sam as they all sat down to hear the board's decisions.

The president looked at Samantha and then over at Mrs. Edwards and Principal Jennings. "First things first. Miss Carter, I am sorry that you had to be treated in such a way by your former principal and his cousin. While we respect your decision to hand in your resignation, it is our wish that you will reconsider and at least finish out the school term."

Samantha looked at Ben, who smiled broadly.

The president then turned his attention to Mrs. Edwards and Principal Jennings. "Mrs. Edwards. It is your decision whether or not to enroll your son in one of our schools, but you will make that choice with the knowledge that we reject the rumors you've spread about Miss Carter."

"Well, I'll not be enrolling my son here! We'll move somewhere else first," Mrs. Edwards shouted. "I can't believe—"

"Mr. Jennings." The board president interrupted Mrs. Edwards's outburst. "We will not be hiring you for the principal's position you applied for or for any other open position in our school district. We believe Miss Carter's and Miss Rogers's testimonies about what happened in Kansas, not to mention that we've had a report from the superintendent of your former school, and he will give you no recommendation. We do not wish for you to be in a position to treat any of our teachers in the manner you treated Miss Carter. This meeting is now adjourned."

"What!" Jennings jumped to his feet and yelled, "You'll believe that little—why, you'll be sorry!"

"Enough! I think the Guthrie school system can do without the likes of you two. Marshal, will you escort Mr. Jennings and Mrs. Edwards out of here?" the board president requested.

Samantha was immediately picked up and swung around by Ben. Before her friends could surround her, Ben said, "We have something of great importance to discuss. We'll be right back."

"Ben—" Samantha looked back at everyone as Ben steered her back to the room they'd waited in earlier. Everyone smiled and seemed quite happy to wait.

Ben had no more shut the door than he turned to her and drew her into his arms.

"Now, will you give me an answer?"

"An answer?"

"To my proposal. Will you marry me, Samantha?"

"But there's no need to rescue me now, Ben. I—"

"Don't you see? It's me needs rescuing, Sam. I love you with all my heart, and I want you to be my wife. Do you think you could ever—"

Joy, pure and sweet, flooded Samantha's heart. He loved her. "Oh yes, Ben Thompson! I already *do* love you. I've loved you almost from the moment you saved my life, and I will be honored to become your wife."

Ben bent down and captured her lips with his. Samantha stood on tiptoe and responded, letting him know that she meant every word she'd said. He lifted his head and looked down into her eyes.

"And I will be blessed to be your husband. I want to meet each new sunrise with you in my arms." They both ignored the knocking on the door as he bent his head down for one more kiss.

epilogue

December 20, 1890

Samantha stood behind Annie as they waited for Rose's signal to start down the staircase. It was hard to believe that this day had finally come. Ben had wanted to get married right away, but the school board had talked Samantha into working through the rest of the term. After she explained that she wanted to have a wedding dress made, along with a few other outfits, and she wanted a few things to bring to her new home, Ben had given in to the delay.

Ben had busied himself with sprucing up the house they would share. Samantha, Faith, and Rose had been out several times to take measurements of windows for new curtains, deliver and supervise the hanging of them, and discuss what new items Sam might want to add to the furnishings. Rose hadn't had time to really furnish the home before her husband had passed away, and then she'd had no desire to live there alone. She seemed overjoyed that the house her husband had built was going to become a real home.

"Are you nervous?" Annie turned and asked.

"A little. But mostly I'm excited. I can't wait to finally become Mrs. Ben Thompson."

"Well I assure you, he thought this day was never going to get here," Faith whispered from behind Samantha. She was too far along to be part of the wedding party, but Sam had insisted that she help her get dressed. Now she stood behind everyone, waiting for Rose to give the signal that all was ready downstairs. "When we heard you come downstairs this morning, it was all Gabe and Matt could do to get Ben out of the house before you reached the kitchen."

Samantha giggled. She could picture Ben insisting on seeing her. She really wouldn't have minded, but Rose and Faith had insisted that he couldn't see her until she walked into the parlor.

"You look beautiful. And you'll know you are when you look into Ben's eyes."

Samantha's stomach fluttered in anticipation of seeing the man she was going to marry. Finally, at Rose's nod, Samantha followed Annie down the stairs and into the parlor, where she passed the boarders, Mr. and Mrs. Miller, Mr. and Mrs. Connors, and Hope and Matt before she reached Ben and Gabe, who stood in front of the fireplace along with the preacher.

She barely recognized that the others were there because her eyes remained fixed on Ben from the moment she entered the room. The light in his eyes drew her nearer to him, and she couldn't keep from smiling as Annie took her place on the other side of the minister just as Sam reached Ben's side.

Faith had been right. The look in his eyes told her he thought she was beautiful, and Samantha thanked the Lord above for bringing him into her life.

As they said their vows, Samantha's heart filled with so much love for Ben she was certain it overflowed to include everyone in the room.

"I now pronounce you husband and wife. You may kiss your bride, Ben."

Ben bent his head and tipped Samantha's face to his. "I love you. I can't wait to see the next sunrise with you," he whispered, right before his lips claimed her as his wife.

Samantha couldn't wait either. She had a feeling that, very soon, sunrise was going to become her favorite time of day.

A Letter To Our Readers

Dear Reader:

In order that we might better contribute to your reading enjoyment, we would appreciate your taking a few minutes to respond to the following questions. We welcome your comments and read each form and letter we receive. When completed, please return to the following:

Fiction Editor
Heartsong Presents
PO Box 719
Uhrichsville, Ohio 44683

1. Did you enjoy reading *Sooner Sunrise* by Janet Lee Barton?
   ❑ Very much! I would like to see more books by this author!
   ❑ Moderately. I would have enjoyed it more if

   _____

   _____

   _____

2. Are you a member of **Heartsong Presents**? ❑ Yes ❑ No
   If no, where did you purchase this book? _____

   _____

3. How would you rate, on a scale from 1 (poor) to 5 (superior), the cover design? _____

4. On a scale from 1 (poor) to 10 (superior), please rate the following elements.

   ____ Heroine   ____ Plot
   ____ Hero   ____ Inspirational theme
   ____ Setting   ____ Secondary characters

5. These characters were special because? _____
_____
_____

6. How has this book inspired your life? _____
_____
_____

7. What settings would you like to see covered in future
   Heartsong Presents books? _____
_____
_____

8. What are some inspirational themes you would like to see
   treated in future books? _____
_____
_____

9. Would you be interested in reading other **Heartsong
   Presents** titles? ❏ Yes ❏ No

10. Please check your age range:
    ❏ Under 18   ❏ 18-24
    ❏ 25-34   ❏ 35-45
    ❏ 46-55   ❏ Over 55

Name _____
Occupation _____
Address _____
City, State, Zip _____
E-mail _____